LOVE WITHOUT ASTERISKS: NEW YORK STORIES

By

Judy Pomeranz

Library of Congress Cataloging-in-Publication Data

Pomeranz, Judy, Love Without Asterisks, fiction
Summary: novella of interlinked stories around the Manhattan art world

ISBN: 978-1939282231

Published by Miniver Press, LLC, McLean Virginia
Copyright 2013 Judy Pomeranz

First edition October 2013

For the man I love without asterisks. Always have and always will.

Table of Contents

Chapter One: Sunday After Sunday After Sunday 1

Chapter Two: The Liquidation...19

Chapter Three: All Partied Out...41

Chapter Four: Another Monday Night..57

Chapter Five: The End of the Evening...73

Chapter Six: Empty Glass, Empty Bottle, Empty Pill Case 91

Chapter Seven: Love Without Asterisks 109

Chapter Eight: Send in the Clowns...127

Chapter Nine: A Huge, Perfect, and Destructive Thing............................143

Chapter Ten: I Can't Do This Anymore...159

Chapter Eleven: A Life's Work 171

Chapter Twelve: There Are Some Things You Can't Do In Eternity.....187

Chapter Thirteen: Finding the Essence 203

Chapter Fourteen: Your Wife is a Very Lucky Woman 217

Chapter Fifteen: I've Done it for You..233

Chapter Sixteen: I'd Like You To Have This..243

Chapter One: Sunday After Sunday After Sunday

Sunday, September 18, 2005

Isabelle would never get used to being here. No matter how often she came, the same feeling of darkness descended upon her when she stepped out of the taxi into this forlorn neighborhood on the western edge of Chelsea. Though she had inhabited the small island of Manhattan for seventy-nine years, she felt like an alien in this part of town, as if she were on foreign soil or indeed perhaps another planet. There were only six blocks between Fifth Avenue and Eleventh, and just forty very short ones between 61st and 21st, but this place had absolutely nothing to do with anything Isabelle knew to be real. It was as if she had crawled off into a dark corner of her own mind, into an illusory or imaginary place. It was always like this.

The broken bottles and shards of colored glass, piles of brown dog feces, stray bills of lading that had blown over from the nearby docks, candy wrappers, cigarette and cigar butts, and the occasional skittering rat all bore witness to the fact that people walked these streets, people lived and worked and maybe even played nearby. But when Isabelle came here

1

on Sunday afternoons, she rarely saw a soul except the drunk who inhabited the doorway of the abandoned body shop next to the lofts.

She was puzzled and oddly saddened, as well as a little frightened, by this tattered man who seemed to be the most constant feature of the neighborhood. He lived out of a shopping cart from Bed, Bath and Beyond and spread glossy fashion magazines across the stoop he apparently considered his home. He wore heavy wool sweaters with the sleeves cut off, and had black skin that disintegrated into flakes as white as the Easter lilies at St. Patrick's. When Isabelle walked up the short sidewalk to the lofts, she reflexively held her breath against the smell he emitted – a combination of urine, cheap alcohol, and a peculiar body odor that reminded her of cooked cabbage...or was it cauliflower? It was not an altogether horrible smell but an ineffably depressing one.

Today the man slept. Though he twitched and mewled softly like a trapped animal, Isabelle considered herself fortunate, because when he was awake his vacant yet penetrating stare drilled a ragged hole right into her chest that left her feeling exposed and vulnerable.

* * *

She had come here every Sunday for the past seven months, and her weekly routine never varied. She woke up without an alarm at 8:30,

2

ordered coffee from room service, showered, dressed, took a few moments to read the Arts section of the Times, and headed for eleven o'clock mass at St. Patrick's, going on foot if the weather was fair and by cab if it was inclement. Mass was more habit than spiritual experience, more ritual than prayer, but it was important to her. It had meant something to her late husband, not that he was ever able to articulate exactly what, and had come to represent a fundamental part of the fifty-four extraordinary years they had spent together. It therefore remained a fundamental part of her life afterwards, a life measured in years she didn't wish to quantify.

After mass, Isabelle would return to the suite at the Hotel Pierre on Fifth Avenue where she had lived since her husband died. She read the front section of the Times and one Shakespeare sonnet; she limited herself to one a week to avoid the possibility that they might become stale or she might become maudlin. Then she refreshed her lipstick and made sure her hair remained neatly secured in a low bun before heading downstairs for brunch at the Café Pierre.

Todd, the maitre d', always seated her in the rotunda, a magical little space with a trompe l'oeil sky on the ceiling and pastoral murals on the curved walls. Though only a few steps up from the main dining room, it was quieter than down below and the tables were further apart. Isabelle liked sitting near the archway overlooking the lower area so she could watch who came and went, and with whom. It's not that she knew them – for the most part they were strangers, probably tourists – but she liked imagining who they were and what they were up to.

Who was married, she always wondered, and who was with a paramour? In either case, would the relationship last? Which of these people came to places like this routinely, and for whom was it a very special, once-in-a-lifetime experience? Who liked art and music, and who invested on Wall Street? Who had pets? Who had children? Who gambled? Who had nasty addictions? Who had had cosmetic surgery? Who lived in the city, and who in the country? Who rode a bicycle or a horse? Who played tennis or golf or dove out of airplanes on the wings of a parachute? Who truly engaged with life, and who merely consumed oxygen?

None of it was important; most of her reflections were not even deliberate. It was simply what she did, how she occupied her mind while she ate her shirred eggs and toast. Sunday after Sunday after Sunday. It was how she kept herself from thinking about other things.

Then, when brunch was finished, she would head for Chelsea.

* * *

"Excuse me."

Isabelle was startled by the soft, male voice she heard behind her as she turned the key to open the door to Jake's 21st Street studio. She'd only rarely encountered anyone in the halls of this building, and never had exchanged words. Not in seven months of Sundays.

"Are you his grandmother?"

She straightened up and turned around to see a tall, pale, fine-boned man of about thirty, she guessed. He was clearly addressing his question to her, but she didn't answer.

"You must be Jake's grandmother," the man persisted. "He talked about you all the time. I believe you were his favorite person in the entire world."

The man spoke these remarkable words without a touch of sarcasm; he spoke them matter-of-factly, a little shyly, and with the barest hint of a southern accent.

"Jake was my grandson," she replied cautiously. "Who are you?"

"John Taylor," the young man said, tentatively offering his hand, which she took, but only briefly. "I was Jake's neighbor here. That's my studio." He gestured to a doorway across the hall, a few feet down from where they stood.

Isabelle nodded. "Nice to meet you." She pushed the door to Jake's studio open and started to walk in, then looked back to find John Taylor still standing there gazing at her with light green eyes that matched the green and white striped shirt he wore with his pressed khakis. He seemed out of place in this part of town.

"He was a wonderful man, your grandson," John Taylor said. "I'm so sorry for your loss."

"Thank you," Isabelle said automatically. "Were you friends?"

"We used to chat from time to time," John said. "He was an amazing artist. So talented."

"You're an artist too, I assume?" Isabelle said.

"No, I write. I use my studio for writing."

Since John Taylor didn't appear to be going anyplace, Isabelle felt compelled to say, "Would you like to come in?"

"Are you sure? I don't want to interrupt anything."

The thought that there might be anything to interrupt was laughable. All Isabelle ever did when she came here, week after week, was sit and think. She did those things here which she was afraid to do anyplace else. She'd look at Jake's paintings, she'd look out the window, she'd look at his still-rumpled bed, and sometimes she'd run her hand over

6

it. She did it softly, reverently, careful not to disturb any of the creases or what she imagined to be his body image in the bottom sheet. She'd think about Jake and his father and his grandfather. She'd see his lopsided smile and the lovely, contented expression that always graced his face when he visited her. She would also see the melancholy that suffused his features when he talked about his father.

"I can assure you you're not interrupting anything," she told John Taylor.

* * *

From the day he was born, Jake had been her favorite. She knew it was inappropriate to make designations like that when it came to linear descendants, but there it was, and no one had to know.

He had been a sweet and glowing child in every way, much more like Isabelle's second son, William, than like Jake's own father, Harold. His skin was soft and lovely, so pale it was nearly translucent. And his eyes had shone from the moment they first opened. They were alert, curious, lively and always twinkling. The twinkle reflected the pure joy this little boy found in the most ordinary things. He delighted in bringing gifts to his "gammy," as he called her throughout his twenty-five year life, despite his father's best efforts to get him to use the more "respectful" and "dignified" term, Grandmother.

When he was a tiny child, he had brought her sticks, handmade clay figurines, crayon drawings, and once a dead mouse. When he a teenager, he brought her irises and brownies, Jane Austen novels, and pretty plastic buttons he found in junk shops. Once, when she had been too sick to go to mass, he brought her some aspirin in a beautifully-painted bottle, pills which made her feel better so quickly she knew the cure was not the medicine but Jake's presence.

When he was a young man, he had presented gifts of delicate, terra cotta figurines, and tiny, silvery sculptures made from twisted wire. He also offered up immense abstract paintings filled with brilliant colors, lush textures and an energy that derived in some part from their slashing diagonals and dancing, sinuous lines but in far greater measure from the life and animation with which Jake had imbued everyone and everything around him.

Each time he brought her one of his works of art, Isabelle had marveled at the mysterious roots of creativity, for she was quite certain no one in her family had ever before created beauty. They had created industrial products, railroads, banks, piles of securities, scores of legal

8

theories and a few diagnoses, but no one other than Jake had ever created beauty.

* * *

Isabelle invited John Taylor to have a seat but didn't know what to do next. She had no food or drink to offer, no entertainment or even scintillating conversation, for her days as a hostess – a role she had approached more as a calling than an avocation – were far behind her. Once renowned for giving the best parties on the Upper East Side ("bar none," said *New York Magazine*), Isabelle now found herself sitting with a guest, of sorts, on a paint-spattered sofa in Chelsea, shifting awkwardly and trying to segue from an uncomfortable introduction to a graceful goodbye so she could be alone, as she was every Sunday. As it was supposed to be.

She watched John scan the room, his eyes skipping from canvas to canvas, and running across loose figure drawings that lay atop rectangular, folding tables which also held jars of oil, cans of turpentine, pads of paper, rolls of canvas, wooden palettes encrusted with dried paint, coffee cans stuffed with brushes, shoeboxes filled with pastels, and wide-mouthed Ball jars crammed with colored pencils. His eyes stopped when they reached the rumpled single bed in the corner of the brightly sunlit studio.

"Do you stay over here sometimes?" he asked.

9

Isabelle shook her head.

"So, the bed's been that way since he...since he was here?"

She nodded very slowly, staring at the floor.

"Would you like some help cleaning up? Or cleaning out? I mean, I'd be happy to help you get some of this stuff packed up or moved out or, or whatever you want. Can I do something to help?"

"I don't need any help," she said with finality. "But thank you." She glanced up at him. "It's very kind of you to offer."

He nodded, then turned his attention back to the canvases. "He really was a fabulous artist. I've never seen pictures with as much passion as Jake's. God, what I wouldn't give to be able to do with words what he does with paint."

"What do you write?" Isabelle asked, just to be polite.

"Short stories," John said.

"About what?" What had started as common courtesy turned into a touch of curiosity; Isabelle had always enjoyed short stories.

"All kinds of things, really. They're mostly set in the south and have what I think of as a southern sensibility. That's about the only commonality among them, I suppose."

"Are you from the South?"

"Born and bred in South Carolina."

"What brought you up here?"

"I went to law school at Columbia and just sort of stayed on."

"I thought you were a writer."

"I write when I can, but I practice law with a midtown firm to pay the bills. Writing's what I do because...I was going to say because I love it, but it's more because I feel compelled to do it. I guess I have some things I want to say."

"Do you live in midtown?"

John nodded. "East 58th Street, off Park. I work at 49th and Park."

"And you come all the way down here to write?" Isabelle was becoming fascinated by this odd young creature.

"I need the solitude, and I love the stimulation I get from the creative people around here. It's an amazing neighborhood and an amazing building. My fiancée thinks it's crazy. She doesn't understand why I write, never mind why I have to come down here to do it."

Isabelle was surprised to hear there was a fiancée. She had assumed this gentle young writer was like Jake.

* * *

11

Jake had been twenty-two when he told his family he was homosexual, or "gay," as he had put it. He had gathered his father and mother, his older brother and younger sister together at home and told them first.

"He's on his way over to tell you," Isabelle's son Harold had seethed when he called her after Jake's announcement. She knew from the way Harold spoke in a near whisper and through lips she could tell were barely parted that he was trying mightily to control his volatile temper. "I wanted to warn you."

"Thank you, Harold." Isabelle tried to keep her voice conversational. "I'll look forward to seeing him."

"God damn it!" Harold shouted. "First it's the art thing and now this!"

"He's your *son*," Isabelle said weakly, knowing she risked fanning the flames by continuing the discussion.

"God *damn* it!" Harold said.

Isabelle understood that her eldest son loved his children in his own oppressive way, but he simply didn't have the capacity to allow them to lead lives that differed in any fundamental way from the one he envisioned for them. Jake had already disappointed him by going into art instead of joining the family investment banking firm. It was a decision Harold had deemed petulant and rebellious, never considering it might have simply been one which Jake made for his own reasons, wholly unrelated to annoying his father. And now this.

She knew how Harold felt about homosexuals, and she knew why. He had learned his intolerance from his father, Isabelle's own beloved husband Carter, who had in many ways been the most generous and caring man imaginable but who could be cruel to those different than he. She was grateful her younger son, William, was more open that way, but often wondered how two brothers could be so different from one another.

When Jake arrived at Isabelle's suite that same evening to deliver his news to her, he told her his father had demanded that he go to the Foster Institute in Massachusetts for "the cure." It was a place Harold's firm had sent employees and associates with similar "problems."

"But Gammy," Jake had said, "there's not a cure for this. It's me. It's who I am."

Isabelle had neither agreed nor disagreed. She had simply given Jake a small kiss on his right cheek, wrapped the beige cashmere scarf she had given him for his twentieth birthday more tightly around his neck, and reluctantly let him go back out into the cold night.

"So, you have a fiancée," Isabelle said to John Taylor. "When are you getting married?"

John paused before responding. "In...in December. Christmas Eve."

"What a lovely time for a wedding." Isabelle imagined bridesmaids in red velvet sheathes and the bride in an ivory silk Vera Wang gown carrying a bouquet of white roses punctuated with sprigs of holly.

John looked at the paint-spattered concrete floor. "I'm a little scared," he said quietly.

"Oh, everyone gets scared as the wedding approaches," Isabelle replied. She wondered why she was jollying this stranger along when the fact of the matter was she had spoken very few extraneous words to anyone since Jake's death.

"She's beautiful," John said, "and very sweet."

"I'm sure she is," Isabelle said.

"And I love her." John said.

"Which is why you're marrying her," Isabelle said, hoping she didn't sound as impatient as she was beginning to feel. She wondered if John Taylor was protesting his adoration a bit too much.

14

"But I don't think that's enough," John said.

"What's not enough?

"That I love her."

Isabelle was unsure of her next line. "It is if *she* loves *you*," she ventured.

"She loves that I'm a lawyer and that I'm smart and good at what I do. She likes my partners and my Hermès ties. She loves the life we lead in midtown, and she loves who I am when I'm there. But she doesn't understand what I do when I'm here or why I do it. She doesn't know this is becoming more and more what my life is about, and I don't know how to tell her."

"Why are you telling *me*?" Isabelle asked.

John thought about the question for a while. "I don't know. I guess because you're here, and because I don't know you, and because I'm comfortable in this place. I used to talk to Jake about things." He pushed a hank of fine, blonde hair off his forehead in a gesture that seemed reflexive rather than necessary.

Isabelle looked out the window at a maple tree that was beginning to turn red.

"Honestly, I don't think I'll ever get over his death," John said. "He was such a good friend, such a good human being. I can't imagine how hard it must be for you. Your own grandson."

Isabelle stiffened, and didn't say a word. She hated this conversation.

"You seem so strong, so resilient," John went on, apparently oblivious to her discomfort.

Isabelle's hands clenched into tight fists.

"I've seen you here on other Sundays, and you always look so stoic, so together, so fine. I honestly don't know how you hold it all in. It's none of my business, but I'm here if you want to talk."

"Would you leave now?"

"I'm sorry...." John said.

"Please leave."

"Forgive me," he said. "I didn't mean...."

"Now."

He got up and went to the door, turned around and said, "It was nice meeting you. And I really am sorry." He closed the door softly behind him.

Isabelle felt violated, as if her personal space had been invaded, almost as if she had been raped or robbed. Her lower lip trembled, but she took a deep breath and pulled herself together. She remembered when a college boyfriend whom she had loved very much told her she was too guarded, too tough for him. He asked if she had ever let herself cry about anything, cry in the arms of someone she loved, someone who would let her cry and cry until she ran out of tears. In some ways the concept had been sweetly appealing, but she knew she could never let go like that, never expose so much of herself to another person, especially someone she loved.

Of course, now she had no one in whose arms she could do that, assuming she were so inclined. But even if she had, and even if she were, she knew that once she started she would never be able to stop the crying.

Chapter Two: The Liquidation

Sunday, September 18, 2005

Larissa let herself into the apartment, grabbed a tumbler from the living room bar, filled it with as much ice and Stoli as the glass would hold, and took a good, solid slug before setting the drink down just long enough to take off her red fox coat and toss it onto the sofa.

She took another, slower sip, then another, before sitting down at the piano and absently plunking out a few melancholy notes, which she recognized only after the fact as the opening bars of "September of My Years." It was a song Sinatra had sung so brilliantly Larissa had never wanted to perform it herself, knowing a comparison would be inevitable and invidious. Her fingers, of their own accord, then picked out the first notes of "As Long as He Needs Me," until she picked her hands up and slammed them down on the keys, creating a cacophony that echoed off the windows overlooking Central Park.

She covered her face with her hands and saw the wreckage as vividly as if she was back there walking through it. She saw the dust and dirt, broken furniture, torn carpet, and drapes half-pulled off their rods, but rather than allowing herself the luxury of bursting into tears she drew a deep breath, raised her head and pulled it together. She detested melodrama and had made a point of avoiding it during her more than twenty-five years as a cabaret singer, which was no mean feat in that profession. The thought that her life might now be defined by that most detested of conceits sickened her.

It made her feel weak and stupid and, worst of all, out of control. This was not how Larissa Sinclair responded to things. The air she affected when performing was that of a woman of a certain age who had experienced all that life had to offer, and experienced it deeply. When she sang about love and loss, pain and rejection, elation and serenity, she made the audience understand that she knew these feelings first-hand; she owned them. She had lived it all and survived, perhaps a little wearily but she had survived nonetheless, neatly and intact.

How many fan letters had she received, praising her soulful and deeply-felt engagement with the world in all its multifarious aspects, lauding her ability to reach an audience member who was suffering and give him or her the strength to carry on? Perhaps her most cherished compliment had come from a sixty-ish man who had sat alone and raptly attentive throughout her act in the cocktail lounge of the Four Seasons Hotel. He approached her when she got up to leave, dropped a hundred-dollar bill onto the piano, and said he could always recognize "an old soul."

"So, you think I look haggard?" she had quipped.

"It has nothing to do with looking haggard, or even old," the man had said seriously. He wore a finely tailored, navy blue, pin-striped suit with a crisp, white shirt. A sky-blue tie speckled with tiny, navy flowers seemed his single concession to frivolity. "A twenty-year old could have an old soul," he said. "It's all about having an understanding of the world that starts with an understanding of oneself. It's about self-awareness, knowing how to live with what life deals out, and maybe keeping a few cards up your sleeve to help you do it. I see those qualities in you and hear it in the way you sing your songs."

Then he had walked away.

While the whole episode had seemed a little cinematic, what the man said had resonated, because it pretty well summed up how Larissa thought of herself. She had been around, as they say; she had opened herself up to what the world had to offer. She had eaten and drunk prodigiously and with abandon; she had lived on the edge of poverty and at the height of luxury; she had trusted everyone and everything and been hurt many times as a result, but she continued to trust. She had loved way

21

too much and far too freely. She had not only survived it all but had thrived. Each experience had made her a more empathetic performer and, she believed, a stronger person. She absorbed and assimilated the good and the bad, the beautiful and the ugly; they all became fundamental aspects of her soul, lending it a profundity and patina that can't be faked.

So, where was that strength tonight? Where was the old soul who knew the score and could handle anything? For the first time in her memory, Larissa was floundering and had no idea how to regain her footing.

* * *

When her therapist had warned her over a year ago about dating a married man, Larissa had laughed.

"I'm not *dating* him, Bernice. That sounds so adolescent. We're *friends*. That's all it is."

"You've been going out with this *friend* pretty regularly now."

"How would you know?"

"Because you talk about him a great deal, and when you do you twinkle."

Larissa laughed again, maybe a touch too heartily. It was a ridiculous word under any circumstances, but particularly absurd coming from her stocky, severe, very beige and untwinkling Bernice. "I *twinkle?* I've been accused of doing many things in my life, but never twinkling."

Bernice responded with one of her hard stares.

"Really," Larissa said, "what are you worried about? I know exactly what I'm doing. I'm simply enjoying the company of a kind and interesting man, one with whom I have a long history. That's all this is about."

Bernice's gaze didn't waver. "I'm worried about you becoming dependent on something you can't control," she said. "Trust me, this is going to hurt."

* * *

Larissa met Bill almost twenty years ago, when she was twenty-three years old and singing in a motel lounge in Jersey City. He had been there with a group of old friends from Princeton for a bachelor party. Amidst clinking glasses, rowdy toasts, clouds of smoke, raunchy jokes and wails of laughter, she had sung a few bawdy songs especially for the party, along with a few of her classic cabaret numbers, then ended the set early because no one was paying any attention. Except Bill.

He approached her as she stood at the bar waiting for Jimmy to mix her a vodka and tonic. "I enjoyed your singing," he said.

"How could you hear it?" she asked.

23

"I guess you have a way of making yourself heard." He stirred his Johnny Walker Black with the little gold plastic sword Jimmy always stuck in rocks drinks. "You have a beautiful voice."

He slurred his words ever so slightly. Larissa knew he'd had a few, but she preferred to think he was still capable of keen judgment.

"Thanks," she said, to Jimmy for the drink and to this man for the compliment. "What's your name?"

"Bill Peretti," he said. "Yours?"

"Larissa Sinclair." She didn't mind telling him, since it was a stage name and not one under which anyone could really track her down. It was only years later, when she realized Andrea Goldman had been completely swallowed up by Larissa Sinclair, that she adopted it as her legal moniker.

"That's a pretty name," Bill said with a gracious smile. "You're a very lovely and talented girl, Larissa. Can I buy you a drink?"

He was so adorable in his navy sport coat and khaki pants, and so different from the pushy, paunchy, middle-aged traveling salesmen who usually populated the lounge that Larissa couldn't bring herself to tell him she drank on the house. He clearly didn't have much experience with this type of establishment, and she didn't want to embarrass him. "Maybe when I'm finished with this one," she said. "Come here often?"

"It's my first time."

No surprise there. "Live around here?"

"Manhattan."

Of course. "What do you do?"

"I'm a resident at Mt. Sinai."

"So, I can call you if I'm sick?" she quipped.

"Only if you have prostate problems. I'm a urologist."

* * *

That was how it all began. In one of the strangest stories she could ever imagine, even more implausible than those in the romantic novels she loved to read, Bill and Larissa, the doctor and the lounge singer, became the best of friends. He was very uptown, and she decidedly Staten Island. He was thin, handsome and preppy, while she was voluptuous and rather exotic, or so people told her. He was smart and rich; she was clever and determined. Together, they pretty much had the bases covered and were somehow wise enough to understand that, but not quite smart enough to do anything about it.

Whenever their equally unconventional schedules allowed them to get together they did, devouring the Big Apple in greedy chunks. They strolled the park, gazed at the moon and adopted a park bench as their

25

own. They window shopped with a vengeance up and down Fifth and Madison, mimicked the animals at the zoo, munched on Zabar's bagels while walking down Broadway, got half-price tickets to the theater, splurged on overpriced drinks at Peacock Alley, and solved most of life's problems in smoky jazz clubs in the Village.

They also hugged and kissed on random street corners, and made the sweetest, most intense love Larissa had ever experienced, in Bill's tiny Morningside Heights apartment. They shared and bared their lives in all-night talks, no holds barred. Naked and vulnerable, is the way Bill described these talks. He told her how he admired yet resented his strict father; how he adored his mother, despite her involvement in the high-society goings-on he claimed to disdain; and how difficult it had been to choose a career in medicine over the family firm. She told him about her estrangement from her family, the abortion she had had at age fifteen, and the embarrassingly high career aspirations she had never admitted to anyone else.

They discussed their respective philosophies of life, as young people are wont to do; they compared values, and marveled at the extraordinary similarities between them. Larissa had no secrets from this man, and wanted none. For the first time in her life, she felt complete. It was all exactly right.

All the while, they both proclaimed that theirs was the purest of friendships. It was an "Aristotelian ideal," Bill had said, a perfect friendship in which each party is interested solely and utterly in the welfare of the other. It was a relationship, they agreed, in which neither had a stake, an agenda, or an ax to grind. They would live for each other and for now. There were to be no expectations; there was only today. They both understood this.

Larissa had lived long enough even then to know that perfection, if attainable, is not sustainable, and that "ideal" is sometimes defined in different ways by even the best of friends. She also knew that the American class system could be every bit as rigid as the Indian caste system. She was not naïve.

Still, a tear had rolled down her cheek at Bill's wedding to his beautiful, well-educated and well-bred high school sweetheart, a tear shed not entirely out of joy for her ideal friend. The wedding was an event both had implicitly recognized all along as an inevitability, given the reality of the way things worked where Bill came from. But it was an event Larissa had mostly managed to put out of her mind during their fourteen months of ideal friendship.

Bill had pulled her aside during the reception at The Plaza and begged her not to be sad. "I'll always love you, Larissa. I promise you that. Our friendship will never, ever change."

But of course it had. It wasn't long before Bill moved to Greenwich, joined a practice in Stamford, and was ultimately lost from Larissa's view of the world. Though she never forgot her ideal friend she was able, in time, to go for hours and sometimes even a day at a stretch without thinking about him.

* * *

Larissa later married once, briefly, more out of loneliness than love, and she quickly discovered the life of a lounge singer did not lend itself to the nurturing of a relationship. So, for most of her life she was essentially alone, though there were many lovers. Her life was busy and full, at least full enough that if it was empty there was no time to notice.

Her career progressed, and she moved from Staten Island to Brooklyn to the Village to Columbus Avenue to Riverside Drive before ultimately landing at an elegant co-op on Central Park West. By that time she was what one might call a star, though she thought the designation sounded déclassé and a little seamy. Still, whatever one termed it, she was known, a name. She sang at the Café Carlyle, Feinstein's, and the Oak Room at the Algonquin. She headlined in tiny cabarets and major venues around the country and, yes, even the world. She had done Carnegie Hall four times, but didn't like to say so because it implied she was counting.

Life was very satisfying, very good. But in the end, she always had to come back to her beautiful, empty home.

* * *

One of Larissa's favorite venues in all New York was Bemelmans Bar at the Carlyle Hotel. She liked the dark intimacy of the place, the warm wood paneling, the whimsical murals that made her feel young and innocent, and the casual ambience. Unlike the true cabarets, Bemelmans was really just a high-class lounge. Its patrons didn't come for the music, and she understood that. The music was simply background. It was a place that reminded her of the early days, the days before they came to see *her*, the days when she was merely a piece of the environmental mosaic, no bigger than any other piece.

She liked the idea of quietly osmosing into people's existences, of her music oozing into their pores and becoming part of their psyches while they were occupied with other things. Unlike most of her professional colleagues, she was not offended by performing in a place where people chattered, laughed, and sometimes cried, where they didn't even know who she was. She was just the piano player who sang a few songs. It was a slice of life, as far as she was concerned, and one that occasionally pleased her.

She enjoyed popping into Bemelmans after the regular entertainer knocked off for the evening. She would sit down at the piano and play, without being hired...or even asked.

That's what she had been doing the night Bill walked in, two years ago now, give or take. He came into the room with another man while she was performing "They Can't Take That Away From Me." Though it had been close to two decades since they had last been together, she recognized him as soon as she saw him. He was as lanky and gangly as ever and still had the peculiar spring in his step that had always allowed her to recognize him from a block away on a dark street.

He and his companion walked to a corner table opposite the bar. They sat down and ordered drinks. Larissa watched as Bill's martini and his friend's red wine were served, then she began to sing.

She had barely sung the first line when he turned in her direction. She smiled. He gaped. She winked. He began to smile tentatively, then grinned his familiar grin, the one that made his nose wrinkle and his whole face light up.

He came over to the piano and waited until the song ended. Then he leaned over and kissed her cheek.

"I can't believe I'm seeing you," he said softly. "Do you have any idea how often I think about you?"

"I've heard that one before," she said. "You forget what business I'm in."

He shook his head. "I haven't forgotten a thing about you." He touched her red hair. "My God, it's amazing to see you."

"Who's your friend?" Larissa said, changing the subject out of embarrassment.

"He's a colleague from Indiana, in town for a urology conference at Columbia this week. But he's not what I want to talk about. Can we get together when you're finished here?"

"I'm finished whenever I want to be," she said with more finesse than she felt.

"Let me make my apologies, and I'll be right back," he said. "Promise you won't go away?"

"Here I am," she said.

31

Larissa played a little Sondheim to bring herself down to earth, while Bill went to talk with his friend. She watched the Hoosier gulp his wine and get up to leave, turning in her direction as he walked out the door.

And then Bill was back, standing by the piano.

"Can we go somewhere to talk?" he asked after she wrapped up "Send in the Clowns."

"How about here?"

"Can I buy you a drink?"

It was just like Jersey City.

"Sure," she said. "A Stoli on the rocks."

While he went to the bar, she went to the corner table where he'd been sitting. She munched on a cashew from a bowl the waiter dropped off, and tried to assimilate what was happening. She felt a little numb.

Bill returned with her drink and sat down across from her. "You are beautiful," he said. "God, I can't tell you how amazing it is to see you."

"So you said."

Knowing a thing or two about self-preservation, Larissa tried to keep her emotional distance. She reminded herself of the ending of their very, very old story, and told herself that they were totally different people

32

leading irreconcilably different lives, but she couldn't take her eyes off him, suddenly recognizing the simple act of looking as an enormous privilege.

Bill put his hand on hers. "You know I've always loved you."

She felt her face flush, but she had no words.

"Don't you?"

"How would I know that?" she said.

"How could you not?"

"You got married," she said simply. "To someone else."

"I did," he acknowledged. "And yes," he said before she could ask, "I still am. But, God, I wish I'd been smarter back then. I've never stopped thinking about you."

She once again had no words, but was wise enough to be very, very scared.

* * *

And that had been the beginning or the re-beginning or whatever it was.

The long walks in the park, the shared meals, the endless conversations, and the laughs all resumed as naturally as if no time had passed, though the walks were now in little-traveled parts of the park, dinners tended to be in dark, out-of-the-way places, and the meetings that used to be in Bill's scruffy Morningside Heights apartment were now held in room 335 at the tony and very discreet Hotel Bristol on the Upper East Side. They both knew too many people in Manhattan to take chances; in fact Bill's mother, Isabelle, lived at the Pierre, right across the park from Larissa.

Each time Bill and Larissa got together, they revealed more of themselves, sharing special or ordinary bits that defined who they had become in the years they had been apart. Bill called the process "opening files." Rather than rushing, as Larissa was initially inclined to do, fearing every second would be their last, Bill taught her to take her time. As the months went by, she gradually learned to trust that after each goodbye there would be another hello, and she slowly allowed herself to overcome her innate skepticism enough to recognize that this might possibly be the once-in-a-lifetime, everlasting love she had sung about for all these years but until now had never really believed in.

She fully recognized that this thing they had was what the world would call an affair, and she suffered pangs of guilt when she allowed herself to think of the wedding she had attended. But she was able to push those feelings down because Bill assured her that his marriage had long been effectively one of convenience and, more importantly, that what they

34

felt for each other was absolutely pure and foreordained, like something that always was and always would be. She felt like a Sondheim realist living a Gershwin song and had the good grace to be embarrassed about the sappiness of her emotions and the feebleness of her rationalizations, but it was what it was, and it made her exceedingly happy. Way too happy.

* * *

"We have to talk," he had said when he called last week.

"Is everything all right?"

"Yes, but we have to talk."

Larissa was hardly naïve. She recognized the words, the tone and the pattern. Over the past six or eight months – since around the time of his nephew Jake's death – Bill had been coming into town less and less frequently; their twice or thrice weekly meetings had gradually diminished to about monthly, a circumstance Larissa had tried to write off as necessitated by schedules. But she couldn't dismiss the distance she felt growing between them, or Bill's guarded demeanor, something she'd been afraid to address or even acknowledge.

"So, let's talk," she had responded, trying to sound casual, trying to keep the tremor out of her voice.

"I'd rather do it in person," he said.

"When?"

"I'm not sure exactly when I'll be in town. I'll call you."

Some things never changed.

* * *

"Did you hear the Hotel Bristol's gone out of business?" Jean-Luc spoke softly but excitedly, as if revealing a closely guarded secret, while he carefully snipped at the ends of her hair.

Larissa's hairdresser knew everything that was happening on the Upper East Side long before anyone else, and he made sure everyone in his circle understood that.

"No," she said, feigning disinterest, "I hadn't heard."

"It was all very abrupt," he said in a dramatic stage whisper. "Seems they've been having financial problems for some time." He peered around to see if anyone else was tuned in on the conversation. "And guess what. They're selling everything in the place."

"Really?" A knot grew in her stomach.

"Really, my dear," he said dramatically. "A liquidation sale." He drew out the syllables, savoring his revelation. "I was over there yesterday and picked up some fantastic bargains. Can you believe a mahogany highboy for $150 and the sweetest little French secretary for $75? I even

36

picked up some cream silk drapes with the most precious tassels for $35. For that, you can afford to have them cut down and remade."

* * *

Larissa walked over to the Bristol the following day and, sure enough, a sign on the front door said the hotel was closed and everything on the premises was for sale.

The interior looked like a war zone. The lobby was piled high with end tables, beds, chairs, TV's, framed prints, and lamps. Larissa could hardly maneuver through it all to the elevator area where folding tables were stacked with wine glasses, vases, silverware, and the distinctive gold and white porcelain the hotel had used for room service.

She made her way into the elevator and got out on the third floor. The corridor was filled with gritty dust. Moldings that had been ripped from the walls littered the floor, a leather-covered phone book was tossed into a corner, and *Do Not Disturb* signs were scattered everywhere. As Larissa walked past the open doors, she saw rooms that appeared to have been ripped apart by a tornado. Mini-bars sat where beds belonged, dirt and grime had settled on all stationary surfaces, drapes were piled on chairs, and carpet was torn up, exposing concrete floors.

The door to room 335 was closed, and Larissa knew she should leave it that way. But she turned the knob, half-hoping the door would be locked, and pushed. When she saw the room, she tried to draw a deep breath but couldn't.

For right there, in the midst of the debris and destruction, she was sure she saw a clean, shiny, gold and white cup, filled with steaming coffee, sitting on the round table between the sofa and armchair. It was on the exact spot where Bill had always put his coffee when they read the paper together in the morning. He would sit in the armchair, coffee at his right; she would sit on the sofa, coffee on the long table in front of her. As they passed sections of the paper back and forth, Larissa would imagine what it would be like to live with Bill and always do these little everyday things together.

Every so often, Bill would peer over his tortoiseshell reading glasses and grin at her. "What did I ever do to deserve you?" he'd whisper.

The wall to the right, where the bed had been, was now blank except for a single walnut night stand, the one upon which Bill's watch used to lie beside her own gold earrings. She remembered how sweetly poetic the vignette had seemed the first time she saw those little bits of herself and of Bill lying side-by-side.

But now tears ran down her face as she surveyed the wreckage one last time. The coffee cup and jewelry had of course disappeared, but the symbolism of the devastation in the wake of Bill's call – the utterly ridiculous metaphor of it all – was far too plain and excruciatingly timely, even for a realist like Larissa. She bit her lower lip, slammed the door and headed across town to her apartment.

Chapter Three: All Partied Out

Sunday, September 18, 2005

Phillip smoothed his shimmery red leggings and pulled on his black jack boots; he donned a silver-spangled tunic, tossed a red ostrich boa around his neck and, on impulse, stuck an iridescent peacock feather behind one ear for dramatic effect, as if more drama were necessary. He spun around twice as he surveyed himself in the mirror. Gloves, that's what was missing. His hands trembled as he pulled on the black leather ones with half-fingers, before declaring the ensemble complete.

But the brilliance of the outfit made his face, adorned with only a hint of foundation, look a little blah, so he sat down at his dressing table and dragged a kohl pencil across each of his eyelids. Then he smoothed some cream blush onto his cheeks, patted on a touch of loose powder, and applied a bright red lipstick that, happily, matched the boa perfectly. Reds could be so difficult, which is why he decided to go with his natural brunette hair color this evening. At least it was his natural color last time he'd noticed, but who really knew what was natural anymore?

He was no Liberace, he mused, thinking about the pianist's beautiful long eyelashes and wavy black hair as he teased his own into a higher bouffant, but it was as good as he was going to get. He popped a couple of red pills into his mouth, loving how they matched his outfit, and washed them down with Bombay Sapphire. Then he put a few spares into his Lulu Guinness "Put on Your Party Face!" bag before tossing on his black satin cape.

* * *

Phillip was in perpetual motion; he never slowed down. Though he technically lived in New York, he escaped for much of the winter to Anguilla, Rio, Palm Springs, St. Bart's, or anyplace warm, sunny and chic. He loved Monte Carlo, Rome, Cannes, Paris, the Costa del Sol and St. Paul-de-Vence in the spring and fall, and he adored spending Christmas in London, feeling very Dickensian and ever so much the traditionalist at that time of year.

Wherever he went, he turned heads; he liked it that way, though he recognized the head-turning was not always in the nature of a compliment. How could one not notice the man with the orange dreadlocks, pink fright wig, or cleanly shaved head, depending on his mood? How could you fail to take note of the tall, willowy fellow who swept into a room with chains of

42

gold jingling to announce his entry? Who wouldn't turn to admire the beautiful man who wore leopard skin or latex trousers at parties and nothing more than a tiny jeweled g-string on the world's best beaches?

Yes, Phillip begged to be noticed. He cried to be noticed. And once in a while he just cried. But never in front of anyone. The one constant, the thing Phillip never appeared in public without, was his trademark laugh. The clothes changed (God knows they did, often six or eight times a day), the trappings changed, and occasionally the facial features changed, thanks to the wonders of cosmetic surgery, but never the laugh. As Phillip himself put it, "I am an upbeat soul and," he would add with a loud laugh, "I am the soul of upbeat!"

* * *

"I love you, love you, *love you!*" Phillip shrieked, as he threw his arms around Lila outside the restaurant Aureole. "You are such a doll to pull this together, *mon petite chou.* I do *not* deserve you!"

"You only turn fifty once, my friend," Lila said, as she pulled herself out of his embrace and held him by the shoulders at arm's length. "You're okay with it all, aren't you?"

"My God, yes!" Phillip said, punctuating the phrase with an exclamation point, as he did nearly everything he said. "I *love* a party, and I *adore* being the center of attention. You know that, my dear."

"You're okay with being fifty?"

"Beats the alternative, as they say," he declared with a loud laugh.

Lila let her hands slip from his shoulders down his arms, and she took both his hands in hers. "Okay, then let's get in there."

* * *

Phillip had known Lila longer than he'd known anyone. They had met the day after he arrived in New York when he was only seventeen, an age so tender he could now hardly bear to think about it. Posing as an eighteen-year-old, the first and surely the tamest of a long series of personae he would take on during his life, Phillip had landed a job washing dishes at a deli in the Theater District, where Lila had worked as a waitress. Though she was three years older and a student at Barnard, the two of them immediately hit it off.

"There's something vulnerable about you, Phil," she had said late one night over her third or fourth glass of wine, "and I find that very sweet. Most guys are so damn ... what's the word? I can never think of words when I've had too much wine...."

44

"Macho?" he said.

"Macho," she agreed. "They're so damn tough they act like nothing can hurt them. In you I see a little bit of a crack."

He had no response.

"You don't mind that I said that, do you, Phil?"

He shook his head, glancing up at the red and white illuminated Budweiser sign over the bar.

"*Are* you vulnerable, Phil?"

He knew she was drunk enough not to need an answer, so he evaded. "I don't know, Lila. There's no reason I would be, I guess...or wouldn't be. I'm no different from anyone else."

That was the most wishful of thinking. In truth, Phil knew he was entirely different from everyone else, which is why he had left boarding school in Illinois and come to New York in the hope of finding a place to blend in. He wanted to hide in the vast crowds, become part of the enormous city masses, and lose himself.

He wanted to become so anonymous, the way people reputedly did in New York, that no one would notice him. No one would care that he existed, not even, most importantly, himself. And for a while it had worked. He had wrapped himself in a conventional image and gotten lost in the hordes of humanity that populated the island of Manhattan. He worked hard at the deli and pounded the streets when he was off, letting the lights and grime of Times Square, the blaring horns, the rushing, pushing, jabbering crowds, and the golden aura that surrounded the boutiques of Madison Avenue transport him to a place where Phil didn't exist – a magical place that obliterated everything but itself.

But before long, the magic wore off. Once he became accustomed to the sensory overload of Manhattan he became inured to it and was back where he started, back to where he had been in Illinois. Back to being part of the regular crowd, which left him with far too much time to think.

That's why he became Phillip instead of Phil – that and the trust that fortuitously dropped into his lap upon his maternal grandfather's demise. It may not seem like a big deal, the transition from Phil to Phillip, but it was huge. Phil was ordinary; Phil was run-of-the-mill; Phil didn't have the edge. Phillip was a character, a personality, a star. Phillip was someone who managed to bury Phil under his aura, his laughter, his wild clothes, and his new nose.

Phillip rarely slept. He never read, and he never watched TV unless he was utterly desperate. He didn't much enjoy the theater or art galleries, truth be told, but being seen in such places was part of the

46

persona. He didn't have a job or what you might call a hobby, and he didn't like activities that allowed his mind to wander onto things he couldn't bear to think about, so he never spent a waking instant alone. At least not if he could help it.

So, what did he do? He traveled the world in good company, usually paying for the privilege, he hosted big dinners, threw parties for the glitterati wherever he happened to be, and he ate and he drank...those things he did with abandon...and of course he shopped. That's what he truly lived for, if he lived for anything. Prada in Florence, Armani in Rome, Cartier wherever, Bulgari in Geneva, Harry Winston on Rodeo Drive, Bergdorf's in New York (for one-stop shopping), and even Burberry in London, once they learned about *red* gabardine and came up with the clever and edgy Prorsum line. Everything in the universe was better when he wore bright colors, sparkles, and fine fabrics.

Phillip was a smothering, all-encompassing being who never stopped moving, changing, and dancing through life on a cloud of beautiful things and pharmaceuticals, a being who made Phil disappear, once and for all.

* * *

Phillip strode into Aureole with Lila on his arm and bowed dramatically when the eight tables of birthday celebrants stood to cheer him. He was so used to paying for everyone's dinner that he was touched and actually quite amazed to be attending a party given for him.

He adored Lila tonight, more than ever. She was the only one who knew him well enough to understand what this would mean to him. Everyone else bought the act; everyone else thought he was as carefree and happy-go-lucky as he appeared. But he knew Lila was onto him, even though neither of them ever said anything. He liked to think of it as their own little Don't-Ask-Don't-Tell policy. He sort of hated that she could see through his veneer but also found it somehow comforting.

"My darling Charles," Phillip crooned to his favorite hair stylist. "How perfectly charming of you to come! And Charlotte," he said, kissing the Frenchwoman's cheek, "I'm absolutely thrilled to see you on this side of the Atlantic! You are too, too much, my dear!" And so it went. He greeted one and all with flourishes and affectionate banter and always, always that laugh.

But far too soon after downing their petits fillets, haricots verts, Dauphinoise potatoes, and chocolate crème brulée (truth be told, Phillip still had frankly Midwestern tastes in foods but loved what French names did for them), the group began to disperse. Chad and Joyce had to get back to the Hamptons; Arturo had a cast party at Sardi's ("How deliciously retro!" Phillip had laughed); Madalena became ill from too much food and wine; Samuel was exhausted from a long day on Wall Street; Henry and Beau just wanted to be alone; and so it went, off they all drifted. Even Emmanuel, on whom Phillip could always count when he needed company, begged off...something about an early morning appointment with his shrink.

"So, my dear, I guess it's down to us." Phillip flung his arms around Lila and planted kisses in her wavy blonde hair. "This was the most delicious evening of my fifty years."

Lila chuckled, which Phillip understood to mean she knew his life was composed largely of a series of such delicious evenings.

"Really. It was so special...all of it," he said. "You know how I *adore* being the center of attention."

"That I do," Lila said.

"The least I can do is take you for a nightcap," he said. "I'm in the mood for the piano bar at the Pierre. How about you?"

"I'm sorry, Phillip, but I've got to run. Andrea's home this weekend; it's Yale's fall break and I've hardly said hello to her."

Phillip felt a familiar hollowness in his stomach when he realized he was on his own, much too early in the evening, but he couldn't keep Lila from her daughter.

"Are you going to be okay?" Lila asked.

"Of course I am," he said with a chuckle, looking out the window at the moon, which he noticed was full. "Don't be silly. I'll be fine. I'll tuck myself in early and be all the better for it tomorrow."

Lila didn't laugh with him.

* * *

Phillip went off to the Pierre alone, and had a few brandies while he listened to a beautiful, redheaded woman sing sad songs. Anxious as always to buy some company, he gave her a fifty and asked her to sing "Cabaret," which she graciously did, but she was plainly in no mood to chat. So, Phillip had a few more brandies and lost himself in the music, until the bartender told him the place was closing and asked him to leave.

Phillip wasn't sure exactly how he got to his apartment on 86th Street, but once there he chatted with Maxwell, the doorman, until conversation ran out, then took the elevator upstairs. But before he even turned on a light he knew he couldn't stay alone in that vast empty place.

Something made him think about the cozy loft in Chelsea, the one where he had spent all those evenings with the artist he had hoped would be and remain his soul mate for life. Even though he had not set foot in the place since Jake died, he had heard it was still empty and knew it would be more congenial there than here. And he did still have the key, which he always suspected Jake had given him more out of pity than devotion.

He knew being there would make him think of Jake, a concept which saddened and even scared him, but it seemed like something he needed to do. Besides, it gave him an excuse to get outside and walk...and walk and walk and walk.

* * *

By the time he let himself into the loft, his tunic was soggy with perspiration. He told himself it was the weather and the walking but he knew it was really the drugs and alcohol. He was stunned to see that the place was exactly as it had been the night Jake died; everything was right where it belonged. Phillip pulled off his wet clothes and threw on the blue-patterned robe he'd brought Jake from the Ritz Carlton in Bali. He put an Ella Fitzgerald CD into the stereo and poured himself a nightcap. Benedictine. There was something soothing about sipping a drink named for monks. He tried to settle into a monastic kind of peace.

51

He focused on the empty bed with the crumpled sheets that still bore Jake's outline, if you looked hard enough. Now that he was here, he hated the solitude and wished he had the nerve, the presence of mind, and the sobriety to go to JFK and catch a plane to Paris or London or anyplace. He picked up the phone to call Lila but realized it was 3:30 and he would seem pathetic...which he was.

So, he opened the drawer of the bedside table and pulled out the beautiful gold and enamel pillbox he'd left there many months ago. When he was alone, his little pills were the only things that could make his world as beautiful as his clothes. Those little pills could take the blackness and make it brilliant with color.

He walked quickly, almost trotted, to the bathroom and grabbed the cut crystal tumbler he'd brought Jake from Ireland. He filled it with water and gulped down one green pill, then a blue one, another green one and one of his favorite red ones. He put the box into the pocket of his robe and went back to the bed where he sat and waited for the rush, the high, the happiness. He waited for the party to begin.

But instead of a rush, Phillip began to feel sober, even somber. And strangely calm. This was a new effect, but then he didn't usually take four pills at once.

He stumbled over to the enormous window and pretended to observe the stars. But rather than finding constellations, he found only his own reflection. His thin white legs stuck out from beneath the blue robe, his hair looked like a small bush, and his eyes were hollow and ringed with smudges of black. Yes, pathetic.

Down on the street, a young boy stepped out of a taxicab. The boy was about twelve or thirteen, blond, soft-skinned, a tad chubby, and very handsome. As Phillip watched him walk up the sidewalk toward the building, his heart started to pound. Chad.

Phillip swallowed another pill and waited, praying for the blackness to disappear. He wanted the lights and colors to be turned on full blast when Chad caught up with him. Was this really it? Was Chad really going to catch up with him, after all these years of running? Phillip anticipated his arrival with a terror that was softened by a tiny hint of something sweeter.

He tried again to find the image of the dashing Phillip in the window. He needed to see the shiny clothes and bouffant hair, but instead he saw Phil. He saw Phil in a blue jacket with a St. Joseph's Academy coat of arms on the breast pocket. He saw Phil with neatly parted brown hair glued into place with, of all things, Brylcreme.

Phil was fresh-faced with sweet pink cheeks and bright blue eyes. He had smooth skin, skin to die for, Phillip thought, letting loose a little laugh at the irony of it. He wondered if it would be his last laugh, and comforted himself by remembering that he who laughs last is supposed to laugh best. But he suspected the truth of the matter was that he who laughs last simply laughs last.

Phillip reached out to touch the warm, pink skin but found only cold, damp glass. He stayed by the window, drifting in and out, popping pills, and waiting for Chad, who was nearby and would be up here soon. Phillip sat back down on the bed and waited.

And sure enough.

Chad arrived with the daybreak. He wore the school uniform – or the part of it he had been wearing when the headmaster had caught them "experimenting." That's what Mr. Westchester had called it when he phoned Phil's and Chad's fathers. But Phil had known it was love, not experimentation, despite the fact that Chad had seemed more curious than committed and that Phil had had to talk him into it.

Even though everyone agreed this would never, never, never, under any circumstances, ever happen again, Chad's father yanked Chad out of St. Joseph's Academy, saying he belonged in an academically superior school on the east coast. That's what he said so no one would know. But Chad never made it to that school. He only got as far as his family's summer home in Lake Geneva.

The next time Phil saw Chad was at the funeral, and then it was only a picture. The poor boy's face was apparently so distorted from the "unfortunate, accidental drowning," they couldn't have had an open-casket funeral even if the family had thought it appropriate. Which they didn't.

Phil was speechless, literally incapable of forming words for weeks or maybe months. He had loved Chad more deeply, more intensely, than he'd ever loved anyone or anything, and now he was gone. Worse than that, Phil knew his own love had killed Chad, though he never knew exactly how the drowning had happened. He swore he would never allow himself to indulge in that kind of deadly love again.

For all these years, Phillip had run around the city, around the world, and around himself in circles and spirals, partying and shopping and eating and drinking and popping pills and, God yes, laughing, all to keep away from this, to stay a step ahead of his beloved Chad. It had worked for a while, and decades later, when he met beautiful, young Jake, he went so far as to allow himself to contemplate love again. He thought perhaps he could even risk slowing down a little. But as it happened in the end, he had to run faster than ever before, his love now having twice proven fatal.

Now he could stop running. Chad had come for him, and Phillip was sure he saw Jake right behind him. The timing was perfect, for Phillip didn't have the energy to keep up the pace anymore; he was too old and too weary.

He shook the last six or seven pills out of the vial and found just enough energy to lift the Benedictine bottle. He put the pills on his tongue and put the bottle to his dry lips. He drank and drank, letting the honeyed liquid slide down his throat and deliver him to the sweetness of the monastery.

Chapter Four: Another Monday Night

Monday, September 19, 2005

Frank squeezed a wedge of lime into the Perrier, poured a more generous than usual Pinot Noir, and handed the two drinks off to Murray, the waiter, for delivery to the handsome young couple seated at a round table by the wall. Both were blond, both were well-dressed, he in a dark suit, she in a slim, navy sheath; they were the very picture of physical and mental health. Frank found attractive, quiet people like them comforting; they brought an air of normalcy with them, however illusory, which offset the crowd of undeniably well-to-do yet frequently bizarre characters who always seemed to populate the place on a Monday night.

Frank grabbed a bottle of moderately drinkable brandy and a bottle of crème de cacao that had probably been at the bar as long as he had, and set about carefully mixing a Brandy Alexander for Isabelle Peretti, whom he was very surprised to see. She was always in the Café's rotunda for Sunday brunch, but that was about it. In all his thirty years at the Pierre, he'd never seen her in the cocktail lounge.

How long had it been since anyone had ordered a Brandy Alexander? Frank prided himself on knowing his customers, whether he'd seen them before or not. He had an 83 percent record of correctly assessing what a patron would order before a word came out of his or her mouth, and he was actually running around 90 percent tonight. But even he missed this one because, really, who would have thought about a Brandy Alexander, for God's sake? Maybe a Manhattan, or even a daiquiri, but a Brandy Alexander was so archaic there's no way it could have occurred to him. He felt every bit the professional he knew he was as he pulled off this coup of ancient mixology without turning to the manual, which of course he hadn't used in many years. One part crème de cacao, one part cream, one and a half parts brandy, and a sprinkle of nutmeg, which he had Murray bring him from the restaurant kitchen. Yes, he was damn good at what he did.

"I'll deliver this one myself, Murray," he said. "Cover me, okay?"

Frank stepped out from behind the bar to take the drink to a table in the far corner, where Isabelle Peretti sat, looking supremely self-conscious.

"Your Brandy Alexander, Mrs. Peretti," Frank said as he placed the drink and a tripartite dish of chips, olives and mixed nuts (with *no*

58

Brazil nuts, thanks to Frank's special friendship with the supplier) on the round table. "It's a pleasure to see you."

Isabelle squinted a bit, as if she didn't recognize him.

"I'm Frank," he said, helping her out. "I sometimes seat you at brunch, when Todd's off." Frank had been known to cover for the maître d' on the occasional Sunday.

She nodded without saying a word.

"Always in the rotunda, right?"

Isabelle nodded again.

She was damn elegant, Frank thought, in an old-world kind of way. The silver hair pinned back in a bun at the nape of her neck, the aqua knit suit, the perfectly-polished, low-heeled black leather shoes, and the reserved manner. He liked Mrs. Peretti; they all did. While she never really befriended or fraternized with the staff, she was always pleasant, much more so than the few other old biddies who lived in the hotel. So, sure, the personal delivery of the drink was maybe partly about angling for a tip, but it was mostly about just being in her pleasant little orbit, however briefly, and hoping for a chance to make a nice old broad happy.

And she clearly needed it. Frank knew his customers, and he knew as sure as he was standing here that Mrs. Peretti was not the kind to drink alone, especially in a bar. Her somber, sort of confused demeanor suggested that she, like many people who came in here alone on a Monday night, needed to escape from something. Frank hoped that was the case, because the only other explanation he could come up with was that Mrs. P was losing it. And the last thing he needed in his bar was another crazy person.

* * *

Frank had gone into bartending forty years ago, not because he was a lush like a lot of his colleagues, but because he was a people person. Sure, he liked to knock a few back – who didn't? – but that's not what the profession was about for him. It was more about being sort of a shrink, without having to get the degree.

He saw folks at their highest (no pun intended) and their lowest, and only rarely in between, because people tend to hang out at a certain kind of bar and chat up the bartender when something monumental has happened in their lives and they have no one else to share it with. He'd celebrated new babies with fathers who couldn't acknowledge paternity, new books with authors who had no friends to throw publication parties, new deals with out-of-town lawyers, new acquisitions with CEO's who simply wanted to quaff a few without their entourages, new face-lifts with

60

bruised socialites, and new romances with more once-and-future lonely folks than he could count.

But he'd also commiserated a hell of a lot. He'd heard about lost jobs, lost friends, lost spouses, lost lovers, lost time, lost health, lost money, and a host of lost causes. He actually liked the losers best. Happy folks didn't need him; they acted like they were doing him a favor by letting him share in their glory. It was the downers who needed him. They're the ones who had brought him into the profession.

Take tonight, for example. Even though it was early, he could pretty much predict who was going to be crying on his shoulder or screaming obscenities in his ear before midnight. Mrs. Peretti wouldn't be among them; she was far too reserved, way too guarded to start up a conversation with a bartender. That was a shame, truth be told, because the more he watched her the more he knew she needed to talk. She was downing that Brandy Alexander like a sailor, but he knew she'd never order a second. Frank decided he'd give her a little time, then bring her another, on the house, and maybe draw her out a little in the process.

The Korean woman who sat alone and was on her third Cutty wouldn't be coming his way either; she hadn't been off her cell since she arrived. She clearly needed to talk, but not to him. The good-looking

61

couple near the window were fine on their own, as well. He figured the guy's Pinot and her Perrier would hold them for the evening, then they'd be heading home to some cozy little Midtown efficiency. He knew the type exactly.

At the table next to theirs a pale-skinned, raven-haired woman in a shiny gold silk dress was joined at the hip with a fortyish guy in a double-breasted blazer. They were clearly out-of-towners. They'd been sipping rum-and-Cokes, crawling all over each other, and occasionally surfacing to take in the scene around them as if they were at the Bronx zoo or something. No, they wouldn't be coming to him for counsel; they'd probably be afraid of anyone who spent too much time in this place, which actually made a certain amount of sense.

Then there was sweet Larissa, who was in here singing her heart out with her pal Crystal, the regular Sunday/Monday pianist, just for the hell of it (as she herself had put it). Frank knew Larissa could use his counseling skills, but he also knew she wouldn't partake. She looked bad tonight, like she hadn't slept in days. Her eyes were bloodshot, her red hair was sticking out in funny directions, and she wouldn't stop singing the saddest songs. It had been the same last night, and when Frank and Crystal had tried to jolly her out of it she had left without a word. So, no one was messing with her tonight. She'd sing what she wanted to sing, and that'd be that. The crowd here loved her, no matter what.

The fact was, the neediest patrons were, as usual, not sitting at tables or hanging around the piano; they were clustered around the bar. They were putting the drinks away, talking about themselves more and more loudly, and getting ready – Frank could tell – to start dumping their tales of woe or braggadocio all over him.

That was the Monday night pattern. First, they'd talk to each other; that could last for an hour or two, depending. Then, when they couldn't stand even the pretense of having to listen every once in a while, when they'd had so much to drink that only talking continuously about their own earthshaking issues would do, then they'd turn to the bartender. Frank didn't flatter himself that it was him they were interested in; anyone who happened to be standing there would do. But he knew he was better at the job than most, and he took satisfaction in performing a service.

Here they all were, lined up and bending their respective elbows, getting ready to bend his ear. There was Sid Bailey, the Broadway producer who hadn't had a show worth a damn since 1970. He was a known quantity who kept coming back because it was one of the few places where folks treated him like a big shot. He'd be crying into his Jim Beam pretty soon, most likely about his wife who walked out on him a couple of decades ago and hadn't been heard from since. Frank felt like he knew her as well as he knew Sid at this point.

Then there was Gloria, the gal from New Haven who couldn't stop telling people she had gone to Yale, as if to imply that a broad could be hot (which she wasn't) and smart too (which she also wasn't). This was probably her tenth or eleventh Monday night, so Frank was getting to know her and her problems all too well. Most of them centered around a father who was a bastard (of so-far undefined nature), a mother who'd cashed in with a razor blade, and a best friend who'd died of some kind of cancer a few months ago. Frank figured Gloria might have been okay until the friend thing. He knew there were lots of latent loonies out there who held it together until some particular kind of trauma hit – the thing that cracked the camel's back, or whatever they say – then fell completely apart.

The poor guy who was now listening to Gloria looked like an investment banker, and Frank figured he might be the exception who proved the loonies-at-the-bar rule. He seemed like he just wanted to down a couple of martinis, and then he'd go back to work. Frank knew the type; these guys never knew when to call it a day. He'd be dead by fifty. Frank was glad the guy was at least drinking real martinis – with gin and vermouth

64

and an olive, and that was that – rather than one of these treacly, trendy, neon-colored drinks that demeaned the name and the tradition.

At the end of the bar was the man Frank liked to call August Wilson, because he resembled the late playwright. He was a tenor sax player, a damn good one too; he'd played a time or two right here in the bar. August was another kind of exception. He wasn't exactly needy and definitely not loony, but he was lonely. He needed the generic company the bar provided more than he needed Frank or anyone else in particular. He needed to be out and among, as they say. He'd sit here all night and hardly say a word. He'd listen to the music, sip his Aberlour, and grin kind of sweetly when anyone paid any attention to him.

But standing behind August was the one man who actually gave Frank chills, even after all his years in the business. The guy named Mike. He was here almost every Monday night, and he always rambled on about his semipro baseball career, which Frank was certain was in the *far* distant past. He was about six foot four and hugely muscle-bound; he was swarthy, dark-haired, and had arms covered with tattoos. He was actually reasonably handsome, but seemed kind of off. He was always so damn nervous, and he'd constantly glance around the room as if he was seeking someone to challenge. A month or so ago, Frank heard him tell Gloria he was off his medication, which made Frank even more nervous.

"Were you at the gym this afternoon?" Gloria asked him now.

"Hell no," he said in a booming voice laced with sarcasm. "I was home reading Shakespeare."

Everyone at the bar except Frank and August laughed uproariously, as if they could think of nothing more ridiculous and therefore more humorous. That brand of laughter, the kind that went way above and beyond the call of the actual joke, was a sign that the group had put away more than enough and would soon be lining up for Frank's attention.

"'*Course* I was at the gym," Mike said. "What the hell do you think? Where else would I be? I'm here or I'm there or maybe I'm out walking the streets. That's pretty much it," Mike said, and tossed back his aquavit.

Watching him drink that firewater reminded Frank of Van Gogh and his absinthe. He wondered if the drink might actually make Mike crazier than he was on his own.

"I'll tell you, though," Mike said, "I can hardly go into that God damn gym anymore without getting into a fight."

"Why doesn't that surprise me?" Gloria said.

66

Ignoring the dig, Mike went on, "There are so many fags in that place these days it's making me nuts." He slammed his fist down on the bar for emphasis. End of conversation.

But as nutty as Mike always was, Frank had seen a man last night who might actually have been weirder, though in a more benign way. The guy ranked among the most bizarre customers of Frank's entire career: a crazy, strung-out, drugged-out guy dressed in sparkling red women's clothes and sporting a hell of an odd attitude. He had downed Courvoissiers practically faster than Frank could pour them, while he listened – really listened – to Larissa's music. He had even asked her to sing *Cabaret*, not exactly your usual request. He wasn't scary like Mike, just weird. And he made Frank unaccountably sad. He was about the sorriest case you could imagine, and Frank felt like hell putting him out on the doorstep when closing time rolled around. He wondered where the guy was now. He couldn't get him out of his mind.

* * *

"This one's on the house, Mrs. Peretti," Frank said as he smoothly picked up Isabelle's empty glass and set a full one – a double – on the table.

She looked down at the drink and then up at him as if she didn't know what to say, but she wrapped her long, thin fingers protectively around the glass. "Thank you," she said quietly. "You're very kind."

"It's nothing," Frank said. "We like you around here. You're a nice lady."

"Would you like to sit down?" she said, tentatively.

Frank didn't remember the last time anyone had asked him to do that. Talk, yes; sit, no. "Uh, sure. I'd like that." He motioned to Murray to take care of the bar for a few minutes.

"So, tell me, Mrs. Peretti, what brings you down here tonight, and why don't you drop in more often?"

She lifted the Brandy Alexander to her lips and sipped. "Lovely drink," she said. "Thank you again."

It was Frank's turn to be quiet. He knew Mrs. P had something to say, and he wanted to let her say it.

She took another long sip. "My grandson died seven months ago, you know."

"I know, Mrs. Peretti. I read about it in the paper. I'm really sorry." Frank had actually heard about it from pretty much everyone on the hotel staff; it was the biggest news around for a few weeks.

"You know how he died, then."

"Yeah, Mrs. Peretti. It was horrible. No one should go that way."

"No one," she repeated after him, as if learning a foreign language. A single tear crept down her lightly-powdered cheek, leaving a little beige trail in its wake, but she didn't cry - not really. "He had a studio in Chelsea. He was an artist."

"I heard that. I heard he was a good one." The last part wasn't true - he hadn't heard one way or the other - but it was what she needed to hear, so it was Frank's job to say it.

She took a long drink of her Brandy Alexander, which nearly finished it off. "I go there every week...every Sunday. It's like I can feel him there."

"That's nice, real nice."

"No, it's not nice. It's a nasty neighborhood and a very silly thing to do - maybe worse than silly - but it's something I seem to need."

"Then there's nothing silly about it," Frank said.

She looked at him with clear, penetrating blue eyes - not the kind of eyes Frank was used to seeing around here - and she went on. "I was there yesterday, as usual."

Frank nodded.

"And someone almost died there last night."

"What do you mean?"

"A man was found there – the police told me about it because I own the studio." She studied the people in the room as she spoke. "I bought it for Jake because his parents didn't approve of him being an artist; they wouldn't support him...my own son wouldn't." She took another careful sip. "The man they found there was almost dead from pills and alcohol. They took him to the hospital. He might be dead by now."

"Jesus, Mrs. Peretti, that's terrible. What was the guy doing there?"

"I don't know. Some woman in the building heard a moaning sound and went to the studio and found him. She called the police. By the time they arrived, the man was quiet, unconscious." Mrs. Peretti wrung her hands lightly, as if washing them. "They said they found a key on him, a key to the studio. So, I don't know. Maybe he was a friend of Jake's...or something. They asked me if I wanted to press charges for trespass. I didn't know what to do, since he had a key, so I said no."

She finished off her Brandy Alexander, and Frank was torn. He couldn't signal Murray for a refill, because Murray would never figure out how to make that retro drink, but he couldn't get up and leave her either. So, he signaled Murray for a plain brandy...the good stuff.

70

"A friend of your grandson, huh? Wonder what he was doing there."

"I have no idea," Isabelle said, trying too hard to enunciate. The alcohol was beginning to show in her speech, but she thanked Murray politely for the brandy. "He wasn't as young as Jake," she said, "but I suppose they could have been friends." She sipped the clear bronze liquid and coughed a little as it burned its way down her throat. "Still, why would he go *there* to take the pills? I don't understand it." Another tear crept down her cheek, tracking perfectly the mark of the first, but her voice didn't even tremble. "There's too much death."

Frank nodded. "Better get the locks changed over there, Mrs. Peretti."

"Too much death," she repeated, then stood up, trying not to wobble. "I think I'd best go upstairs now. Thank you again for the drinks." And off she walked, with some effort but great dignity.

Chapter Five: The End of the Evening

Monday, September 19, 2005

Leaving the cocktail lounge of the Café Pierre, Isabelle walked slowly through the rotunda, past the table she always occupied on Sunday mornings, making her way to the elevators. She stumbled slightly as her left foot tripped over her right. She was certainly feeling the extra drinks the bartender had so kindly but unexpectedly brought her.

She could hardly believe that only thirty-six hours had elapsed since she last sat here eating brunch. It seemed like decades had gone by, as if Sunday morning had been part of another lifetime altogether. And in a way, it had been, for she had since lived through two events that had shaken her in fundamental ways. First, there was the disturbing encounter at Jake's loft with the young man named John Taylor, and then this morning's call from the police telling her about the man named Phillip who had almost died in that loft.

Drugs and alcohol, they had said.

Not unusual, they had said. Happens all the time.

But who was the man named Phillip, and why would he have done what he did?

And why in Jake's studio? *Why there?*

And then, of course, this evening Isabelle had found herself in still another new situation: sitting all alone in the hotel bar, a place into which she had never ventured in all the years she had lived at the Pierre. Even though, given everything, she could understand what might have provoked the strange compulsion to go out and have a drink, the fact was she had never before sat alone in a bar and had very rarely exceeded her limit of two glasses of wine. Tonight she'd had at least three harder drinks, maybe more, all alone.

And why had she talked to the bartender about Jake and about this man called Phillip? Why had she, Isabelle Peretti, who had been strong when her beloved husband Carter had died and stoic when young Jake was killed, told it all to a bartender? She was always the person people talked to, not the one who talked.

She carefully negotiated the steps down from the far side of the rotunda and headed for the elevators. She punched the button and waited. It had indeed been an unusual thirty-six hours, a period that had left her feeling utterly unmoored. Or maybe that was the alcohol.

74

Carter, a man who had drunk far more than Isabelle thought healthy but was able to handle it with no evident ill effects, had often said that drink didn't modify one's feelings in any fundamental way but simply magnified them. If you loved someone, for example, you'd adore them after a couple of drinks. If you were sad, you'd be bereft. If you were at sea, you'd be lost.

* * *

John Taylor was quite sure it had been her, Isabelle Peretti, Jake's grandmother. He'd seen her sitting by herself near the door of the Café Pierre, a couple of tables down from where he and Natalie sat. Mrs. Peretti had been drinking some kind of creamy brown drink and talking with the bartender. John assumed she must be a regular.

He gently took Natalie's hand and squeezed it as they left the bar and turned off Fifth Avenue onto Sixty-First Street. It was a clear, cool evening, and he liked the idea of being out late at night in the middle of the city. It was energizing, and he always got his best story ideas when he was walking the streets. That's why he, unlike Natalie and most everyone else he knew, shunned iPods and cell phones when he walked; it's also why he usually preferred his own company to that of others.

"But what are you going to *do*?" Natalie would often ask when he headed out for a late night stroll.

"Walk."

"But to where? For what?"

"I just want to walk. Walk and think. And if I get lucky, I might see the moon."

She sometimes acted as if she didn't believe him, didn't trust him, as if she thought he was hiding his real destination. Other times she looked at him as if she thought he were a little off.

But tonight, as they turned to walk down an unusually quiet Park Avenue, she squeezed his hand back.

"Are you excited about the wedding?" she asked.

He smiled, hoping that would be enough of a response.

He wondered what Isabelle's marriage had been like, what her life had been like. She seemed very sweet, and he supposed she had to be for Jake to have been so crazy about her. But she was also a little prim, a little restrained, as if she was afraid to fully engage with the world, as if life had maybe let her down one time too often.

"What are you thinking about?" Natalie asked.

"Not much," he said, "just musing about some of the people at the bar."

"They were kind of a strange lot," she said. "I would have thought the Pierre would attract a better class of people."

"I thought they seemed like a fascinating bunch," he said, not sure why he felt compelled to defend them. "I got the feeling most of them would have had some pretty interesting stories to tell, if we'd asked."

"But they seemed so scruffy or something. A little...I don't know...down and out, or just down. Not the kind you'd expect to find on Fifth Avenue, certainly not the kind you'd like to spend a lot of time with."

John didn't respond, but he let Natalie's hand fall out of his.

He hoped he hadn't offended Isabelle at the loft yesterday. He sometimes probed a little too deeply, not always sensitive enough to know when to quit. He'd have to work on that.

"How about that singer," Natalie said. "What a skank! All that wild red hair...and the décolleté. I'd say she's been around, huh?"

"I thought she had a nice voice," John said.

"Oh please, John. She was screeching...and the melodrama...all those songs about love gone wrong. Let's just say I don't think we'll have

77

her perform at the reception." Natalie gave a little laugh and tried to take John's hand again, but he pulled it away to brush her hair off her face.

* * *

Larissa walked across the park toward her co-op on Central Park West. Though the fall night air was cool and crisp, she felt ragged and depressed. She wasn't sure why she had decided to sing two nights in a row at the Pierre but knew it had something to do with indulgence. It was not about professionalism or pleasing the audience, not by a long shot; she knew it had been far from her finest performance.

No, it had more likely been about need. Need for diversion, maybe, or for adulation or adoration. Or maybe it was an even more basic need, like purging. It was as if singing sad songs would exorcise the demons of tragic love by pushing them out of her body through her mouth.

"How idiotic," she said in a harsh stage whisper to no one in particular, not caring whether anyone in the park heard her talking to herself. She was disgusted with the self-pity she had been wallowing in ever since her conversation with Bill, a crushing depression that had only been exacerbated by her trip to the Hotel Bristol's liquidation sale. And she was frightened by her inability to control her emotions, crazed by these insane mood swings.

She wrapped her soft gabardine coat more tightly around her and tied the belt.

She always enjoyed being with her friend Crystal, who played the Pierre regularly. They were a great team, Crystal on the ivories and Larissa belting it out, but Larissa knew she'd let her friend down these last two nights. It had shown in their tips, not that either of them needed the money, but it was a point of pride. The only big tip had come from the freaky cross-dresser last night, a man who'd obviously been in even deeper need than she.

Cabaret. That was what he'd requested. It seemed so appropriate that the man with the mad persona and desperately wild attire would pick a number that resonated with wartime craziness and, yes, desperation. He was a man who needed for life to be a Cabaret; a man who couldn't survive it any other way. She knew the type all too well.

* * *

Phillip slowly came to. His head felt like a raging tangle of red hot wires; his mouth and throat were as dry and scratchy as sand. His stomach felt as empty as the crater of a dormant volcano and as unsettled as an active one. His limbs were limp, his bones nonexistent. When he tried to move his arms, then his legs, nothing happened. When he tried to move his hand, only the pinkie lifted.

He made an attempt to take in his surroundings but it was dark, and his vision was distorted and blurred. He peered through a dense gray cloud at hazy furniture that seemed to advance, then recede, then advance again. A small rectangular table, a bedside chest, a vinyl-covered chair, monitors that beeped timidly and flashed. He didn't know where he was, but he was sure it was neither home nor anyplace else he had gone voluntarily, for he would never choose a place with such drab furnishings. Everything was gray or beige, except the walls, which were a quiet but nasty shade of green.

He was able to bend his neck far enough forward to cast his bleary gaze down to his hands. Where were his rings? Where were the Cartier watch and the bangles he never took off? He racked his brain to recall recent events, but without success. This was not what they called amnesia, he felt sure, because he knew who he was and where he was supposed to be; he was Phillip, the king of everything beautiful and gay, and he was supposed to be in a glorious setting, any glorious setting. But he wasn't. He didn't know where he was or how he got here.

But at that moment it didn't really matter, and he drifted back into a peaceful oblivion.

* * *

Isabelle undid the brass buttons of her aqua St. John jacket and hung it in the closet next to the skirt. She peeled off her stockings and tossed them into a satin laundry bag, then looked up at the large mirror on the closet door. She was still slim and wore clothes easily and well, but was not accustomed to scrutinizing herself unclothed and was unsettled by what she saw.

Her skin was wrinkled, creased, and spotted with age; it fell into small folds at the tops of her arms and in her inner thighs. She bent over to unhook her bra and let her breasts fall free. They still had some fullness but had become pendulous since she'd last paid attention, and hung close to her torso. What had happened to her, and when had it happened?

She was diverted from this unpleasant examination by a blinking red light on the telephone. She punched in the number 35 to retrieve the message from the hotel's voicemail system. It was from an officer something-or-other, NYPD. He said Phillip Maxwell, the man who had been found in Jake's loft, was going to be okay. He was in and out of consciousness at St. Clair's Hospital, but he was going to survive.

81

Isabelle sat on the bed and remembered the hours she had spent in a waiting room at Lenox Hill Hospital after getting the call that Jake had been taken there. His father and mother had been vacationing in Amalfi, and Isabelle's second son William had not answered Isabelle's call, so she had sat there alone for a very long time. Jake had been taken into Emergency and from there transferred directly into an operating room. Isabelle had waited in the cold, dingy waiting room until four in the morning, when a doctor came and told her that Jake had died. Knife wounds. In and around the heart. Puncturing a lung. Puncturing the aorta. Puncturing the large intestine. Puncturing the throat. Nipples cut off. Penis cut off. Could she see him? No. You wouldn't want to.

Jake had died alone.

As Carter had. She had left his bedside at the hospice to get a cup of coffee.

And now she was alone. She had her two sons, of course. And they loved her, in their ways, but they didn't need her. Carter and Jake had needed her, and they had loved her more deeply than anyone else ever did or would; of that she was absolutely certain. Now, there was no one in the world for whom she was the most important person.

Is that what love is about, she wondered? Do we need those most who need us most? Do we love those most who love us the most profoundly? She felt an ache in her chest, and wondered if this was what they meant by a "broken heart." It hurt more than she could say to have loved someone so very, very deeply and then to have lost him. Twice.

There was a void, an emptiness, an enormous pit in her center that nothing could fill. She had read her share of Tennyson over the years, and while she often admired his ideas she did not honestly believe it was better to have loved and lost than never to have loved at all. Without love there could be no hurt as great as this, no loneliness as great as this, no feelings of incompleteness or purposelessness or futility like the ones she had known since Jake's death.

Carter had been right about drinking, she realized. It provoked thought, and it did magnify everything. She had been at sea, and now she was lost.

* * *

After John and Natalie kissed each other good night, Natalie rolled over and snuggled into a fetal position. Though John knew this was an invitation to wrap himself around her from behind, he instead picked up *The Great Fire* by Shirley Hazzard and started reading where he had left off, at the point where the war veteran Aldred Leith seemed to be in the end stages of working his way back to his beloved, the young Helen. Perhaps they would not end up like Abelard and Heloise, after all, or like Ms. Hazzard herself whose eternal beloved, a soldier she had met as a young girl, had been killed in the war.

John lay the open book cover-side-up on his chest and looked over at Natalie. Her breathing was already becoming regular. Unlike him, she was a good sleeper; she didn't seem troubled by the kinds of doubts that plagued him. Her blonde hair covered the side of her face and spread across the pillow. John touched it, and she sighed softly. She was a beautiful woman. She was smart. She was in love with him, or at least with a part of him. Why should he have doubts? What more did he want? Was it rational to want what Leith and Helen had, a fiery romance that burned so intensely nothing could put it out? Not disapproval, not distance, not even war. Or was that kind of love only a fictional construct?

Maybe he was a dilettante with his writing, as he often suspected might be the case. Maybe the novelty would wear off, as Natalie hinted it might. If it did, and if he gave her up just because she couldn't understand the part of him he now thought was the biggest and most important, he might find himself a year from now with nothing but a law practice. No wife. No family. Alone.

For some reason, that was not as frightening as he knew it should be.

* * *

Larissa pulled a glass from the freezer and filled it with Stoli Lemon. When she drank alone, quaffing fruit-flavored vodkas seemed less degenerate than downing the regular ones. She collapsed onto the sofa and took a sip. The chill was nice; it complemented the sweet tang of the lemon flavoring. She could almost pretend she was drinking lemonade. This was not about the alcohol, she told herself, it was all about the cheery little taste.

Sure.

She drained the glass and set it on the coffee table.

What was it, she wondered, that made this so different from all her other love affairs that had gone bad, or from all those everyone else talked about? If the world fell apart every time two people called it quits, the whole human race would have disintegrated a long time ago. What was it about this particular experience that made her feel so unhinged, so completely unequipped to deal? Was it the history she and Bill shared, the intense friendship that had preceded the affair? Was it possible that there was actually something to that damn Aristotelian notion that there's really only one person out there who can make another feel truly complete?

Liquor made Larissa philosophical, although her drunken philosophizing was inevitably embarrassing when recalled in the cold, sober light of morning. Still, a few drinks often clarified her thinking, or so she told herself. She poured some more vodka into her now-warm glass.

As still more alcohol pumped through her system, she became a little calmer, and felt a little stronger. She had choices, she thought. She could end it all – everything – right now, to avoid ever facing the possibility of encountering this kind of pain again. But that seemed a bit extreme. Or she could go on with her life but guard against ever again falling in love, thereby improving the odds of avoiding the pain. But that could lead to such a sterile existence that life might not be worth living at all, which circled her back to option one. Or she could move on; she could stop wallowing and start living, which she knew was the most rational of the choices at hand. The only problem was she didn't quite know how to do that.

It was then that she experienced a rare moment of clarity, one of those gifts that sometimes zips right past because we're in too much of a hurry, or too sober, to notice. It was so simple. So damn simple. She didn't have to let him control their communications, as he always had, which made it feel like he was actually controlling her; she didn't have to wallow alone, as she was so used to doing. She actually had nothing to lose at this point by simply picking up the phone and dialing Bill's home number. Which she did.

* * *

Phillip heard someone ask him how he felt. He slowly gained a measure of consciousness and found a blonde woman dressed all in white, standing before him. Being a Tony Kushner fan, Phillip wondered if she was an angel. He squinted so he could see the vision more clearly. No, she was dressed more like a nurse than an angel, a perception he met with mixed emotions. On the downside, it meant he was not in heaven, nor was he probably about to receive a revelation. On the other hand, he was most likely alive, which was, as far as he could recall, a good thing.

"I'm fine," he said, more out of polite habit than considered judgment. In reality, he hurt all over.

"You're going to be as good as new pretty soon," the angel-nurse said. "But you had a close one, my friend."

How nice to have a friend, Phillip thought dreamily. And right here at my bedside when I'm feeling a little punk.

"How do I look?" he said.

"You look fine," the woman in white said.

Phillip looked down at the thin, dingy, blue-and-white striped gown he wore. "Liar," he said with an attempt at a grin. "And I'm sure my hair's a fright."

"You're right about that," the angel/nurse said.

* * *

Frank put away the last glass and wiped the bar clean.

"See you tomorrow, pal," he said to Murray as the waiter prepared to leave for the night.

Frank worried about how long Murray would be with him. He'd been on the hotel staff for forty-eight years, which was a record, and had really begun to slow down in the last few months. He walked so damn slowly, so tentatively, it was as if he was afraid to move, afraid his body wouldn't do what it was supposed to. And he hardly spoke anymore. He rarely said a word to Frank and never spoke to the customers. He'd stand there and wait for them to give him an order, which he'd write on the same kind of pad he'd used for the last forty-eight, then he'd shuffle off to get Frank to fill it.

Frank hated thinking about Murray because he knew he wasn't all that many steps removed from there, himself. He poured a brandy, leaned his elbows on the shiny bar and took in the silent room. He saw the ghosts of the evening's patrons drinking and chattering and laughing. They were like the audience in the George Bellows fight painting Chloe had once shown him, their faces distorted as if they were being seen through funhouse mirrors. Their laughter was screechy, more scream than titter, and their quirky behaviors were exaggerated into full blown insanity. Frank wondered if this bizarre vision might be more real than what he saw when they were all actually there.

When it was quiet like this, after everyone had gone home, Frank had to work hard not to let his thoughts wander too deeply into the dark territory. When the bar was full of these nutty, needy people, Frank had a mission. But after they left, he lost track of what that mission was. Who was he serving here? Of what good were these oddballs to humanity? Of what good was he? Is this all there was?

After thirty years in this place, he knew this *was* in fact all there was for him. There was nothing at home. Just him and a one-bedroom place in the Bronx. There hadn't been anyone or anything else since the leukemia had stolen Chloe from him when they were both twenty-eight.

She had begged him to go on living, to find someone who would make him happy, and he had tried, albeit half-heartedly. For years, he had taken out a woman here and a woman there, but nothing clicked and no one measured up, and in the end Frank had found searching and dating to be depressing and more trouble than it was worth. It'd sometimes be okay for a movie or a drink or even a quick dinner, but that would be that. And in the end, he'd always go home alone.

Chapter Six: Empty Glass, Empty Bottle, Empty Pill Case

Tuesday, September 20, 2005

Isabelle awoke to the glare of sunshine pouring into the room through a gap in the heavy silk drapes she had neglected to fully close. As she gingerly sat up in bed the room whirled around her, a harsh reminder of the brandy she had consumed the night before, but it settled into equilibrium surprisingly quickly. She stepped into her white satin mules and walked over to the window, moving slowly to ensure the dizziness didn't recur. She drew the drapes open.

Central Park shimmered. Sunlight glittered off the ponds, filtered through the dewy atmosphere, dappled the brilliantly colored autumn leaves and glanced off the roofs of cars that snaked along the park's twisting lanes. As she watched joggers, walkers and roller skaters traverse the paths, Isabelle pulled the sash window open a crack and listened to the wind as it rustled through the trees and wrapped around the corners of her building.

The cool, mildly humid air which smelled sweetly of nothing felt soft and gentle as it blew her filmy nightgown ever so slightly, making her strangely but pleasantly aware of her skin. She was suffused with a serenity

91

she hadn't known since Carter's death, and maybe not even before that. She had no idea what the source of this magical feeling was, but she didn't want to leave the window, for fear the spell would be broken.

* * *

Freddie from Room Service brought her coffee at 9:00, as usual. By that time, she had showered, dressed in her favorite red St. John suit, and positioned herself in the blue chintz-covered chair. As she sipped the strong brew, she breathed in its deep, nutty aroma, savoring it as she never had before. Common sense, with which she was well endowed, would suggest that her new appreciation of caffeine was mostly due to last night's overindulgence, but it felt like more than that. It was as if she'd gone from ignoring or even fearing the sensory intrusions of the world to welcoming them, if timidly.

She tried to read the morning *Times*, but couldn't concentrate on crime statistics, Iraq, Mayor Bloomberg's campaign to clean the streets, or the blockbuster exhibition at the Metropolitan Museum. Her life was more interesting than the news, she thought, recalling the man they had found in Jake's loft. The man who'd almost died. The man they called Phillip.

Not so very long ago, Isabelle would have been wise enough to leave the matter alone. After all, it was none of her affair; she was only involved because the loft happened to be in her name. She had no reason to care about this Phillip person or to pursue the situation any further. From what she'd been told, no harm had been done to Jake's studio, so why not let it rest, pretend it had never happened?

* * *

At 10:35, Isabelle stepped out of a taxi in front of Jake's building, fascinated by how animated the Chelsea neighborhood was. She'd never before been here on a weekday, and was amazed to see people rolling up graffitied steel shutters on what she had thought were abandoned buildings to reveal the stark white walls of art galleries. She was taken by the number of people walking dogs – tiny, yapping ones and enormous, lumbering ones – and impressed by how well-dressed the people were and how civilized the whole scene appeared. It was all so unlike her Sundays.

Even the man who lived on the stoop of the building next door had become an enterprising businessman. He had pushed his blue plastic shopping cart out to the sidewalk, stationed himself beside it on a milk crate, and placed a Styrofoam cup in front of him. A very tall, slim man dressed in a perfectly tailored light beige gabardine suit bent over and

93

stuffed a bill into the cup as he passed by. Isabelle heard him greet the street man by name. "Good morning, Sam," he said.

Sam. For some reason, Isabelle was surprised the man had a name, or one that hadn't gotten lost in the shuffle of whatever had brought him to this place in his life. Sam. He still smelled vile; he was still raggedy and scabrous and dissolute and filthy, but he had a name. He had a name, like Harold or William or Jake, a name some mother had chosen for him when he was a tiny baby.

When she reached the front door of Jake's building, she turned around and took a last glance at the man called Sam before putting her key in the heavy metal door.

* * *

The atmosphere inside the building, as outside, was charged with an energy Isabelle had never experienced on her Sunday visits. Most of the doors were either ajar or fully open to the hallway, exposing artists' studios filled with paints, metalworking tools, pottery wheels, looms, stone-cutting implements, video cameras, and works in progress of all sizes and types. Music spilled out of several doorways, mostly jazz tunes of a sort Isabelle had become vaguely familiar with through Jake and her son William, both of whom loved the form.

94

The hallways smelled of fire, oil paint, turpentine, alcohol, coffee and sweat. Discreetly peeking into doorways as she walked by, Isabelle found most of the artists to be alone, but one or two worked in partnership with others, setting up a banter that further enlivened the space.

When she got off the elevator on Jake's floor, she noticed the door to John Taylor's studio was closed. She wondered if it was because he was hard at work at his midtown law firm or if perhaps he was in there creating a short story. She was embarrassed and a little ashamed, recalling her petulant departure from him on Sunday. Why had she been so defensive? The young man had merely been making conversation, after all. Or had he really been overly intrusive?

She opened the door to Jake's studio and peeked in, fearful of what she would find there. She moved slowly into the room, leaving the door ajar. Although the police had assured her there was no apparent damage, she feared finding any evidence of another person that might dilute or obliterate the continuing presence of her grandson, which she had always been able to conjure in this place.

The bed was still rumpled, maybe more so than usual. Isabelle leaned over it and tried to find the outline of Jake's body, but it was gone, obscured by the general mess of covers. She tried, as always, to smell his sweet little-boy scent in the sheets, but instead she smelled the acrid odor of old liquor. Then she saw the dry, brown stain on the sheet that was the smell's source.

A blue robe lay on the floor near the window; that was new. And an empty glass, a drained Benedictine bottle, and an enamel pill case sat on the bedside table.

Overdose of alcohol and drugs. That's what the police had said. Apparent suicide attempt, or possible criminal stupidity. That's what one officer had told her, with a snide chuckle. No one seems to know why he was there, ma'am. Maybe the door was unlocked and he just happened in. I'm afraid I can't help you out on that one.

Empty glass, empty bottle, empty pill case, and a brown stain. This was all she knew of the man called Phillip.

* * *

After the locksmith had come and gone, Isabelle left the loft. She stopped on her way down the hall and knocked softly on John Taylor's door, not knowing what she would do if he answered. She would probably apologize, she thought, and then be on her way. But a part of her wanted to help the young man who had been Jake's friend. She had sensed in him the same kind of desperation she had occasionally sensed in Jake himself.

96

It was a sort of frightened, unsettled feeling that accompanies the knowledge that to do what you need to do to satisfy your own deepest yearnings you may have to upset those you love, and relegate yourself to the margins of what you have always been taught to believe was mainstream society.

While she never liked to think about it, Isabelle knew Jake had lived with that feeling nearly all his life. He had died with it. She hated the thought of another young man suffering that way.

* * *

"Good morning, Sam," she said stiffly, trying out the man's name. Holding her breath, she snapped open the brass clasp of her black leather pocketbook, took a twenty-dollar bill from her wallet, folded it up and placed it in the Styrofoam cup.

Sam squinted up at her and nodded. "Thanks."

Isabelle thought she saw something approaching intelligence, or at least awareness in his face. "Why do you do this?" she asked, surprising herself with the question.

"Why do you do what *you* do?" Sam asked.

It was a question Isabelle had never allowed herself to address. She knew Plato had contended the unexamined life was not worth living, but she had always feared that the examined life might be revealed to be unworthy of living. On the rare occasions she had been tempted to allow her thoughts to go in an examining direction she had pulled back, telling herself there was no time for such folly or frivolous mental machinations. But she knew it wasn't really about time; it was about fear of being revealed inadequate. She didn't know how people gathered the courage to engage in deep introspection or psychotherapy. The very thought terrified her.

She looked into Sam's watery red eyes and at the stubble of black beard on his chin that had something linty and white stuck on it. A blistery lesion dominated his forearm, crusted spills marred the front of his ratty beige sweater, and his brown leather shoes had their toes cut out. She wondered whether this odd fellow might address the question she asked him, and the one he asked her, throughout much of the day. Indeed, what else would he have to think about as he sat here all day long? She appreciated his not pressing her for an answer.

"I don't know why I do what I do," she said quietly, then walked to the corner and hailed a taxi.

* * *

"His name is Phillip," Isabelle told the receptionist at St. Clair's Hospital. I don't recall his last name."

98

"I'm afraid I can't help you if that's all the information you have." The woman wore a pink smock that marked her as a volunteer. Isabelle had spent enough time in hospitals to know the type.

"He was admitted because of an overdose of drugs and alcohol."

The volunteer perked up at this. "Oh," she said, elongating the vowel to imbue the word with the greatest sympathy. "In that case, he'd either be in intensive care or on the psych ward." She scrutinized Isabelle, as if to ascertain whether she might have driven the poor man to his fate.

"Can you see if you have a Phillip in either place."

"I'm not really authorized..."

"I'd greatly appreciate anything you can do for me," Isabelle said in her most formal tone, arranging her features into the saddest face she could muster. People rarely turned her down when she really wanted something.

The woman began scrolling through lists of names on her computer monitor. "I have a Phillip Maxwell in ICU," she whispered. "Only family members are allowed to visit."

* * *

"Yes, I'm his grandmother," Isabelle said to the nurse manning the desk in the intensive care unit. The lie came more easily to her than she might have expected. "How's he doing?"

"Much better now. We've got him stabilized and he's going to be fine...physically," the young black woman said. "But he's going to need some serious therapy," she added quietly.

Isabelle nodded. "Therapy. Of course."

"Would you like to see him?"

"Is he up to it?"

"He's been in and out. We've had him pretty heavily medicated and sedated, and he's still dealing with some of the vile stuff he put into that poor system of his, but he's allowed to have family visitors."

"Has he had others?" Isabelle asked.

"You're the first." The nurse walked Isabelle to a room down the hall and left her outside the door. "He's in here."

Isabelle peered into the tiny room and saw a tall, gaunt man lying in the bed. He was pale and had a shock of messy, thick brown hair that framed his thin face. He was neither good looking nor bad. He was actually quite nondescript, lying in that narrow bed which was cranked up to a half-sitting position. He seemed wispy, as if he were nothing more than a thinly covered set of bones that had fallen where it had been flung. Rather like a bean-bag doll, Isabelle thought. Not like something that would or could move of its own accord.

As she got closer, she realized he was quite a bit older than she had expected him to be. She had assumed he'd be in his twenties, like Jake, but Phillip Maxwell appeared to be somewhere in the vague reaches of middle age. His skin was smooth and white, virtually wrinkle-free, but there was a weariness about him, something that marked him as older, though nothing Isabelle could quite put her finger on.

"And who are you?" he said slowly, as if forming words were an effort. He smiled as he spoke. "I love your red suit. You're the first one I've seen who's not in white, so you must not be an angel."

"Hardly," she said. "I'm Isabelle Peretti."

Phillip's features crumpled as the smile evaporated. "Peretti," he repeated quietly.

They studied one another for a time before Phillip said, "You must be the grandmother."

He started to drift off. "Jake was crazy about you," he murmured.

"You knew my grandson?"

Phillip moved his head again, even more wearily this time. "I loved your grandson."

"Were you ...."

"Lovers?" Phillip filled in the word Isabelle didn't know how to say. "We made love from time to time, but we were never really an item, much to my dismay. But oh my God, I adored that boy." Phillip tipped his head back with apparent effort and looked at the ceiling. "I loved him more than I'd let myself love anyone in decades."

Isabelle didn't know what to say.

"He was a perfect doll," Phillip whispered. "So handsome, so sweet, so damn talented." He inhaled deeply. "Why can't we protect the people we love, or at least not destroy them?" He let out one giant, heaving sob. His shoulders began to shake, and tears poured down his face. "Excuse me," he choked. "I'm really not like this...not...I'm sorry. It's the medication.

"Shall I call a nurse?" Isabelle asked.

"God no," Phillip said. "Don't call anyone. I need to say this." He moaned softly. "And then I need to die, so I won't hurt anyone else."

"Did you hurt Jake?" Isabelle asked through tightly pursed lips.

Phillip's mouth hung open. His deathly pallor and expression reminded her of Munch's *Scream*. "You mean physically?"

Isabelle didn't respond, but sank into a chair. She supposed she meant any kind of hurt.

"Oh God, I would never have a laid a hand on that perfect boy, other than one that was totally loving."

"Then what did you mean about hurting him?"

Phillip leaned his head back against the pillow and took a deep breath. Then another.

"I hurt him by loving him." He said the words slowly, deliberately. "Just as I hurt Chad."

"Who's Chad?" Isabelle asked.

Phillip recounted the story of the first boy he had ever loved, the only one before Jake, the boy who had not truly loved him back but who had died because of his own father's wrath which had been provoked by Phillip's love. It was that simple, he said. Phillip never knew whether Chad had killed himself, or if his father had driven him into the water that day in Lake Geneva, or if the whole thing had been a terrible, horrible accident, but he knew that the whole thing would never have happened if he and Chad had not done what they had done together, what he had tantalized – or dared – Chad into trying.

"And what about Jake?" Isabelle asked, impatient with the story of Chad because she needed to hear about her grandson. "What did you do to Jake?"

103

"I loved him," Phillip said, "and I went with him to the park that night."

"You made him go there?"

"No," Phillip said. He spoke softly now. "It was his idea. But I'm the one who told him about the place, and I was happy to go along with it."

"What place? What was he doing in the park? Why did he go?" Isabelle blurted out the questions that had long haunted her. She knew what the police had said, but she didn't want to believe them.

"I had told him about that corner of the park," Phillip said. "Until I met Jake, it was the only place in New York where I found love, or what passed for love. Oh, I have friends – lots of friends – but after Chad, I was afraid to have a real lover, afraid of what my love might do to him. So, I went to the park and kept it anonymous. I found warmth on cold nights, and comfort when I was sad." Phillip went on, as if in a trance. "I found company when I was afraid to be alone, and solace when I was despondent. It was far from perfect, but better than nothing."

"And what did *they* get, the ones who helped you?" Isabelle asked.

"Money," Phillip said.

"And Jake? Why did he go to that place in the park?"

"He didn't, normally. In fact, he'd never been before. Jake didn't need what I needed. Everyone adored him, and he could have had anyone he wanted as a lover. That's why I could never understand why he chose me, at least occasionally." Phillip let out a small, dry laugh. "I sometimes thought I was the father his own father couldn't be to him. I suppose that's what Dr. Freud would say. Or maybe he felt sorry for me; I *am* kind of pathetic, and he was so good-hearted. I also think he thought I was entertaining. Jake loved anything that was fun and amusing."

Isabelle nodded, remembering that to have been the case. "Is that why he went to the park?"

Phillip nodded. "He thought it would be fun." He ran a hand across his brow, wiping away some drops of perspiration that had formed there. "He was not promiscuous, certainly not in that random kind of way. But we'd had a few drinks, and he wanted an adventure that night, so I took him. I introduced him to that hellish place...and so to eternity." A lonely tear rolled down Phillip's white cheek. Isabelle had never met anyone so dramatic. He seemed like a caricature.

"An adventure," Isabelle murmured.

Phillip nodded.

"But tell me one thing," Isabelle said. "Why did you...befriend Jake, if you were afraid of hurting anyone you got close to?"

"I was completely smitten," Phillip said, turning the drama down and speaking with a deep sadness in his voice. "From the time we met at a gallery opening last summer, I knew I was in love."

Not believing in love at first sight, Isabelle was less than convinced, but still somehow moved by this strange man's apparent sincerity. And by his torment.

"I wanted so badly to befriend, as you say, your grandson, that I convinced myself my penance had been paid in the form of all those loveless years, with a few Hail Marys thrown in as security." He was quiet for a moment. "It had been so long. So very, very long. I allowed myself to enjoy his company intermittently over about six months, and only then learned my debt had not been paid."

Isabelle wanted to hate Phillip Maxwell for putting Jake in the place where he met his death, but instead she felt sorry for him. She recognized loneliness and knew his was of an extreme type and degree.

"Were you with him when he died? Did you see it happen?"

"Oh, my God, no. I read about it in the paper, like everyone else. The last time I saw him he was walking hand-in-hand with a handsome stranger. He seemed very happy. He even winked at me, as if to say his little adventure was turning out to be all he'd hoped it might be.

"Where were they going?"

"I don't really know. I was with someone, too."

"Did you talk to the police?"

"Of course," Phillip said, starting to slur his words. "I phoned them and told them what I knew, but they acted like it wasn't of any use to them. One even told me that people who go to places like that deserve what they get." Phillip's mouth could hardly form words now. "I didn't press. I didn't have the energy. It was too late for Jake, anyway."

Phillip breathed heavily and regularly, then started to snore.

Isabelle sank back into the stiff, vinyl-covered chair. She too was exhausted, and wished she could go to the gentle place Phillip now inhabited.

Chapter Seven: Love Without Asterisks

Tuesday, September 20, 2005

Larissa awoke to a bright, sunny morning, which stung her eyes and reminded her of the quantities of vodka she had consumed the night before. The glaring blue numbers of her digital clock told her it was 6:15. She groaned as the stinging radiated into a dull, aching aura that spread across the crown of her head.

She burrowed more deeply into her feather pillow, pulling up the downy duvet and trying to ignore the churning of her stomach juices. Sleep. That was what she needed; that would take care of everything. Endless amounts of sleep.

But it was too late for that; her mind kept returning to last night's pathetic performance at the Pierre. She recalled the sad expression on Crystal's face when she had had to fill in the words Larissa was unable to sing from *The Second Time Around.*

"What's wrong with you, sweetie?" Crystal had whispered to her when the song came to an end. Crystal called almost everyone sweetie, a mannerism Larissa had once thought affected but later realized was really just Crystal. It was who she was and how she talked. When she called you sweetie it was honestly because she thought you were sweet.

"Nothing's wrong. I'm fine."

"You are not fine," Crystal said bluntly. "Why don't you go home and get some rest. I can handle this by myself."

Of course she could; it was *her* gig. Larissa was only there because she needed to be out and about and doing what she did. She needed not to be alone. Usually when she popped in to sing a few at the Pierre, Crystal was thrilled and the audience loved it. Larissa was a *name*, after all; Crystal was just a lounge entertainer. But Larissa knew she hadn't done Crystal any favors last night.

She hadn't left until Frank insisted it was time to close up, not wanting to return to her empty apartment, her serene seventeenth floor *aerie*, as Bill called it, overlooking Central Park, the place that normally made her happier than anyplace else on earth. Cabaret singers needed solitude when they were off the job, at least Larissa did, and her home was where she normally found it.

But sometimes solitude was the enemy. Sometimes it just made her realize how alone she really was, despite the adulation of the crowds.

She pulled the duvet over her head to block out the light and concentrated on emptying her mind, the way a yogi in California had once taught her. She pondered an empty nonsense syllable, hoping it would consume the turmoil of her thoughts and cancel everything else out. She imagined the OHM filling her head, leaving room for nothing but itself. She imagined it as a clog in a pipe that created a blockade, which would prevent any thoughts from passing through or even filtering around it.

But of course it didn't work; she had never been good at this stuff. Thoughts of last night slammed into the OHM and smashed it into little pieces that were dissolved in the tidal wave of unwelcome recollections that rushed in to replace it.

She vaguely recalled having had a few vodkas when she got home. Lemon. And then the phone call. God. She pushed the duvet down and reached for the bottle of aspirin in the drawer of her nightstand. She tossed a couple back and washed them down with the glass of water she always kept by her bed.

Oh, my God. The phone call.

She got up and walked unsteadily to the window. The park looked soft in the hazy light that filtered through the trees and cast vague shadows on the grass. She wanted to enjoy this view the way she used to. She wanted to take in the splendor of all this nature and feel the peace she used

to derive from it. And the satisfaction. She was a gal from Staten Island

who had made a life for herself, a pretty perfect life. She had been mostly

content since she'd lived here, with just enough heartache thrown in to

make her feel alive and enough sorrow to make her understand happiness.

She had conquered the little corner of the world that mattered to her and

had this ethereal piece of land and sky and Central Park to prove it. And

she had done it on her own terms; she had been in charge.

But since Bill had come back into her life she'd been anything but.

For a while she had enjoyed the off-balance feeling, imagining this was what

true love was all about. Then off-balance led to out-of-kilter which

inevitably led to out-of-control which resulted in desperation and

subjugation to this thing she called love but was really more like an

addiction – one that had culminated in the phone call that proved how

crazy and self-absorbed she had become.

* * *

Larissa walked fast. She pounded down the footpaths of the park

as quickly as her legs would allow. This was what she did when she was

anxious, scared, unhappy, or just needed to escape. She also often drank in those circumstances, but something told her the drinking had gotten out of control, along with everything else. So this morning, she walked.

As she did, she watched the legions of healthy young people jogging and biking through the park, men and women with wiry or heavily muscled frames who made her feel old and slothful. They had clear faces and beautiful skin; they moved with purpose and little apparent effort. They wore tired tee-shirts and plain gym shorts. A few had sweat shirts tied around their waists. Their shoes were sturdy but worn. What they were doing here was not about appearances; it was about something Larissa didn't fully understand, yet somehow admired.

She bent down to take a drink at a fountain and saw her image reflected in the shiny steel bowl. Her eyes were red, and the skin around them puffy and dark. Without makeup, her complexion was splotchy and marred by rosy patches that grew out of the exertion of the walk, but also came from the vodka. Her red hair, still mostly her own natural color, was wild this morning, curling around her head and tumbling anarchically over her shoulders.

As she set back out onto the path, she noticed a pale, thin, vaguely familiar young man jogging in her direction. He gave her a curious look as he passed by, then turned and walked up beside her.

"Aren't you Larissa Sinclair?" he said shyly.

"Yes. Do I know you?"

"No," he said. "But I heard you sing at the Café Pierre last night."

Then it clicked. He had been there with a delicate young woman. They had actually listened to the music. While the others in the lounge had chattered and preened, these two had whispered quietly from time to time but mostly listened, and even applauded. Larissa had envied the relationship they seemed to have.

"I'm John Taylor," he said, still panting a little from his run. "I loved your performance."

"It wasn't one of my best," she said.

"You were wonderful," he said, lifting the bottom of his tee-shirt to wipe the sweat from his face. "I mean it."

"That's very kind."

"I'm not being kind," he said. "I loved the way you sang."

"Thank you," she said. She slowed down a bit and turned to him. "I recall you were with a very lovely woman."

"My fiancée," he said.

"Congratulations."

"Thanks," he said.

114

But he spoke without enthusiasm, and Larissa had been in the lounge business long enough to know that all was not right in this man's world.

"Do you come to the Pierre often?" She wanted to keep him talking, curious about what his story might be and honestly hoping for a diversion from her own ugly self-absorption.

"Not really. We live close by, but we've only been there a few times. I'm usually working at night."

"What's your work?"

"I'm a lawyer. Antitrust."

Larissa nodded, but said, "Funny, I wouldn't have taken you for a lawyer."

"What then?

"I don't know, something more creative maybe. Artist or actor or something."

"Why do you say that?"

"Instinct, I suppose."

"Well, you're not too far off. What I really want to do is write fiction."

"So, why don't you?" Larissa said.

"I've got to make a living," he replied. "That's not easy to do writing short stories."

"Can't your fiancée help out you while you get started?"

"She doesn't take my writing seriously."

"A lot of people didn't take my singing seriously in the early years," Larissa said.

"Really?"

"God, yes. Are you kidding? If you think it's hard telling your fiancée you want to be a writer, try telling her you want to be a lounge singer. She'll beg you to write." Larissa laughed for the first time in days. "I remember telling my parents I wanted to sing – they both worked in factories, mind you; it's not like I was dragging the family reputation down with me – and they thought I was nuts. My father got his cousin to give me a job at a tannery in Maryland so I could make an 'honest living.' I lasted four weeks before I got myself a gig at a godforsaken bar in a godforsaken town in the middle-of-nowhere-redneck-Maryland."

"Hardly the Café Pierre," the young man said, smiling.

"Hardly," Larissa agreed. "But that's where I got my start. I sang sad songs about frustration and loss and love and yearning. I sang about things I knew, and it worked because my audiences knew them too and understood that I sang from experience. That's what it's all about, John Taylor. If you write about things you know and things you feel, and you feel them so deeply that people can't help but understand what you're saying, you're going to be a real writer. And you're going to make a living at it the same way I make a living off *my* feelings. And your girlfriend will see you're good and you're earnest and you're serious, and you'll be on your way."

"You make it sound so simple," he said. "But I don't think my fiancée wants to be married to a writer, even one who's good and earnest and on his way. I think she wants to be married to a lawyer."

The two of them walked quietly and companionably for a while until John Taylor stopped and blurted out, "I don't know why I'm telling you all this. This is really crazy. You're Larissa Sinclair, for God's sake, and I'm droning on about this ridiculously petty stuff. I'm truly sorry, Ms. Sinclair. I really am."

"First of all, my name's Larissa. Second, this is hardly ridiculous or petty. This is your life we're talking about...and someone else's, too. And third," Larissa touched the young man's arm, "I'm a lounge singer; I'm a pro at this love stuff. Remember?"

He blushed – actually blushed – which was really too sweet for words. "Thank you for being so kind. I'd never talked to anyone about any of this until a couple of days ago." He shrugged. "I guess I figured if I didn't talk about it or think about it, everything would be okay. And now, since Sunday, I've told my story to two complete strangers. Pretty crazy, huh?"

"Not crazy at all, John Taylor. We all need to talk, and it's always easier to talk to strangers about things that really matter." Larissa felt like she was playing her shrink Berniece's role, but what she said sounded exactly right and true. "It seems like you have some doubts, and like this relationship might be making you more unhappy than happy, at least right now." Larissa took a deep breath of the fresh morning air, rather enjoying pontificating. "It's possible that this is not the right person for you, or maybe the timing's off, even though you want so badly for this to work out, even though you might have perfect sex and be in perfect sync."

"We're not in perfect sync," he said quietly. "That's what I'm saying."

That's when Larissa realized she'd been talking about herself.

"Can you be a little late for work, John Taylor?"

"I guess so," he said. "Why?"

"How 'bout a cup of coffee?"

That's when Frank, the bartender from the Pierre rounded a bend in the path and walked toward them.

"Hey, Frankie," Larissa said, moving comfortably into her brassy lounge singer persona. "What are you doing out here?"

"What's it look like? I'm walking."

"You don't live around here, do you?

Frank shook his head and buttoned the two middle buttons of his tattered brown v-neck sweater. "The Bronx."

"So, what brings you here?"

"Walking," he said tersely.

"Long way from home," Larissa said, enjoying taunting him.

"I do it every week...every Tuesday."

"Good for you, Frankie. Exercise regimen, eh?"

"Sort of."

"How about joining me and my friend John Taylor for a cup of coffee? Don't even think about trying to turn me down. I know you don't have to be at work for a good long time."

* * *

"Oh my God, this is amazing," John Taylor said, as he took in the sweeping view from Larissa's living room window.

Larissa watched him turn from the view and scan the chintzes and silks, the mahoganies and walnuts, the pure colors of the oriental rugs, the neo-impressionist paintings in gilded frames she had enough taste to know were over-the-top but still loved, and the comfy fullness of the stuffed furniture.

"It's a wonderful place," he said.

Larissa was proud of her domain, and it had been too long since she had shared it with anyone. "Have a seat. You too, Frankie."

Frank plopped down into her favorite yellow-and-white striped chair, but didn't seem particularly happy to be there. Of course, Frank never seemed particularly happy to be anywhere. He never really smiled and never, ever laughed, as far as Larissa knew. He was a very somber kind of guy.

John Taylor sat down on the yellow and blue flowered sofa while Larissa went into the kitchen and flipped on the coffee maker her housekeeper always set up before she went home in the evening.

"Do you like bagels?" Larissa shouted.

"Sure," John Taylor replied.

"Fine with me," Frank said.

"Butter or cream cheese?"

"Cream cheese" they said simultaneously.

"You a New Yorker, John Taylor?" she yelled back.

"I'm from South Carolina."

"Well, good for you for learning how to eat a bagel. If you can pick up localisms that easily, you'll be a fine writer."

She put plates, mugs, napkins, butter knives, sesame bagels, a carton of whipped cream cheese, milk, sugar and the coffee pot on a tray and carried it into the living room. God, this felt good. It felt normal, so pleasurably normal, and she began to realize how long it had been since she'd done anything normal. Between secluding herself waiting for Bill to call, and sneaking around town with him after he did, she'd had little time or energy left for the simple, sweet, normal things people did.

Much as she had loved having Bill back in her world, and as extraordinarily happy as the happy times had been, nothing about her life had felt natural or comfortable since their reunion. There was always the yearning, the guilt, and the feeling that the whole thing was more like one big fantasy date than real life. And there was always the waiting and waiting and wondering and waiting and feeling mildly sleazy in a way that not even singing in Jersey City had made her feel.

All this came into crisp relief as she talked with John Taylor and Frank. Her guests.

* * *

While they munched on bagels and sipped coffee, Larissa told a totally attentive John Taylor about her career. She talked about the dives and the palaces, the amazing highs and devastating lows. She even dropped hints about her short-lived marriage, a subject she rarely discussed, not because it was so painful but because it hardly seemed worth mentioning. There was only one thing she didn't talk about.

She enjoyed keeping this young man enthralled; this is what she was good at. But she was worried about Frank. He seemed even more sullen than usual and had hardly said a word since he'd been here.

"Well, this has been a totally amazing experience, Ms. Sinclair," John Taylor said as he stood up to leave, "but I'm afraid I have to get to work."

"Larissa."

"Okay, Larissa," he said, blushing again. "How can I ever thank you?"

"Shouldn't be too hard. It was only coffee and a bagel."

"You know what I mean," he said, holding out his hand.

Larissa took it, drew him toward her, and gave him a peck on the cheek. This young man brought out maternal instincts Larissa didn't even know she had. "Come back anytime, John Taylor."

* * *

"So, what's up with you, Frankie?" Larissa plopped down onto a chair next to his.

"Nothin'. Same as always."

"You seem a little down."

"You've seemed that way yourself lately," he said, masterfully diverting the implicit question.

"You're right about that, Frankie, and I'm sorry if I scared some of your customers away with my pathetic performances the last couple of nights."

"You were fine."

"Sweet of you to say so," she said. "So, you walk here every Tuesday, huh? Doctor's orders?"

He shook his head. "Personal thing. Just something I do."

"Why Tuesdays?"

123

Frank was acting like a big child who was angry at being grilled by a parent. "You're full of questions, aren't you?"

"Just curious," Larissa said.

"It's because of my wife."

"I didn't even know you were married, Frankie."

"I'm not," he said, looking down at his hands. "But I was."

"And you walk in the park because of her?"

"It's the last thing we did together – I mean really did – before she died, not that it's any of your business," Frank said. "It was a Tuesday morning. Twenty-nine years ago."

"I'm sorry, Frankie," Larissa said quietly. "I didn't mean to pry. I had no idea."

"No one does. It's nobody's business." Frank stood up and walked over to the window.

"I'm sorry."

"She was the best damn woman there ever was," he said, studying the view out the window. "There's never been anyone like her and there never will be again. I know people always say stuff like that because the person's dead and becomes a saint, but it's not like that." He turned to Larissa. "She was a saint even when she was alive. She was sweet and adorable and perfect, damn it. *We* were perfect. No qualifiers, no footnotes, no goddamn asterisks."

"I believe you, Frankie," Larissa said.

"I gotta get out of here," he said. "Thanks for breakfast."

* * *

Larissa sat on the sofa and looked at the impression Frank had left in the overstuffed chair. That's what love's all about, she thought. Cherishing a memory quietly for twenty-nine years, walking with her spirit every Tuesday, and pleading with someone to understand and believe she was perfect.

It made all the games Larissa played with Bill and with her own life seem ridiculous and shameful. When love was really love, both people knew it, and they did what they had to make it complete and honest. No asterisks.

It wasn't about one-night stands and dinners in dark corners; it wasn't about fleeting moments of happiness and weeks of despair; and God knows it wasn't about getting to the point where you could have ruined the life of the person you thought you loved by making a stupid, desperate phone call in the middle of the night and hanging up when the wife answered.

Chapter Eight: Send in the Clowns

Tuesday, September 20, 2005

The shrill ring of the bedside phone woke Bill Peretti out of a sound sleep. He felt his wife Vanessa turn over to pick up the receiver.

"Hello?" she murmured.

Bill's service had strict orders to call his cell when there was an emergency, not the landline. His first thought was that something was wrong with his mother.

Vanessa hung up the phone and burrowed back under the covers.

"Who was it?" Bill asked.

"It was no one," Vanessa mumbled, turning over onto her stomach and embracing the pillow so that it plumped up under her head. "Must have been a wrong number. They hung up."

Bill could see the clock on Vanessa's nightstand, which read 2:30 a.m. Beside it, the still-illuminated number on the phone's Caller ID pad bore Larissa's number.

He lay still, hoping Vanessa would drop quickly back to sleep and praying Larissa wouldn't try again. What was she *thinking*? What was she *doing?* He didn't know whether to be frightened or angry. Maybe she was in trouble; maybe she needed something. She had never called him at home before – never called him at all, in fact. He was the one who did the calling, and it never occurred to him she might try.

As soon as Vanessa's breathing became heavy and regular, Bill slipped out from under the covers and went downstairs to the library. He sat by the phone, ready to grab it if it rang again. Yes, he had to have that talk with Larissa; things simply couldn't go on like this. But he wasn't going to have it tonight, and most definitely not from home.

* * *

At 7:30, after showering and trying to pull himself together for the day, Bill sat down at the table in the breakfast room. He'd been awake since the call. Cupping his mug in both hands, he breathed in the aroma of the strong, steamy coffee and tried to read the Times, but he couldn't stop thinking about Larissa.

"So, what's your day like?" Vanessa asked as she came into the room.

Dressed in a peach silk robe and slippers, her blonde hair mussed from sleep, and her clear, pale face free of makeup, she looked far younger than her almost-fifty years. She seemed small, and vulnerable in a way that

128

saddened Bill. She pulled the Arts section out of the paper, sat down across from him, and without waiting for a response, started to read.

"I'm taking my mother to the hospital," he said.

"What for?" She turned a page, and began scanning the "Arts in Brief" column.

"Her annual physical," he said. "Remember? I told you about it last night."

"Hm."

"What about you?" he asked, wondering why they went through these motions day after day, when neither of them really cared. "What's your day like?"

"Lunch with Molly and Sue at the club, a meeting at Joan's on the Kidney Foundation dinner. Guess that's about it." She turned another page. Even from across the table, Bill could smell the talcum and sleep on her.

They were comfortable together, he thought. There was something to be said for that, maybe a lot. But there was no fire, no intensity, certainly no passion. He wondered if there was love. He was not *in* love; that much he knew; and she wasn't either. He couldn't remember whether they had ever really been in love. But maybe there was some other kind of love between them. Maybe like that which a brother has for a sister, or a friend for a friend. Was there that much caring? Or were they just used to being together, just comfortable with their history and in their well-established habits and patterns, content with the ease and predictability of it all?

* * *

Isabelle's annual physical had become a surprisingly pleasant tradition for Bill and his mother in the years since his father had died. They had a routine. Each year, Bill would join her for a late breakfast at the Café Pierre before walking her to Lenox Hill Hospital. He would get her settled into her room, then spend the day strolling the streets of the Upper East Side, an activity he loved but hadn't done enough of in recent years. He would check back in on her before dinner, then dine with a friend (in the past two years, the friend had been Larissa) before going back to spend the night at Isabelle's place (though in the past two years, he'd spent the night with Larissa at the Hotel Bristol).

Isabelle would be finished and ready to leave the hospital by the middle of the next day. Bill would drive her home, get her settled, and head back to Greenwich. These two days of the year constituted something of a mini-vacation for him, one which Vanessa had never shown any interest in joining him on, and that was actually fine. Bill enjoyed the feeling of freedom he had walking the city streets on his own and without a mission. And he enjoyed the casual time with his mother. It was a nice change from the relative formality family visits seemed to take on when Vanessa was with them, visits during which everyone seemed to be on their best behavior.

"Good morning, Mother," Bill said as he walked into the Pierre's 61ˢᵗ Street entrance. He was surprised to find her waiting there rather than upstairs in her suite.

"You look exhausted," she said.

"Thanks, Mother. Nice to see you, too," he replied with what he hoped sounded like good humor.

The truth of the matter was she looked exhausted too, and more melancholy than usual. Bill didn't want to upset her by saying anything about it, which was pretty much in keeping with the way the family communication dynamic had always worked, so he simply asked, "are you ready for your appointment?"

She nodded. "I suppose so, though I can't say I'm in the mood to go to another hospital."

"Another?"

"I visited a...an acquaintance at Saint Claire's yesterday. It was a very long afternoon."

"Who's at St. Claire's?" The West Side hospital was hardly on his mother's beaten path, or that of her friends.

"It's a long story," she said.

"You can tell me at breakfast," Bill said as he took her arm to walk her to the restaurant.

* * *

"I was awake most of the night," Isabelle said. She closed the menu and began fidgeting with her heavy white damask napkin.

"Why? What's wrong?"

"I'm not sure. It's just been the strangest couple of days."

Bill didn't respond, not wanting to break the spell that seemed to be making his mother actually talk to him about something that mattered.

"You know what they say about the ripple effects of an event, about how many different lives can be affected by a single thing?"

Bill nodded.

"Lives of people you don't know, people you never even imagined were in the world...all affected by a single, terrible event." Isabelle spoke as if in a trance or a dream, as if she were talking to herself.

132

"What event, Mother?"

"Jake's death," she said slowly. "A man named Phillip tried to kill himself in Jake's studio on Sunday. The police called me."

Bill still couldn't hear his nephew's name without feeling like someone had punched him in the stomach. "Why didn't you tell me, Mother? I would have come --"

"There was no reason to tell you," she said, interrupting him, "and I'm not talking about me. This man was a friend of Jake's. He was in love with him." She paused until the waiter finished pouring their orange juice. "He's tormented, William. He feels responsible for what happened." Isabelle's voice shook. "He took Jake into the park that night and introduced him to a place where men...find other men."

"How do you know all this?"

"I visited him in the hospital."

"Why?"

"I'm not sure. It felt like the right thing to do. I can't explain it."

"Mother, you really shouldn't --"

"Stop it," she said firmly. "I'm old enough to do what I want and frankly tired enough of this life not to worry about what might happen to me."

133

"Do you think this guy might have been involved with Jake's death?"

"No, I'm certain he wasn't; that's what I'm trying to tell you. He's devastated by the whole thing. And he's not the only one. I met a young man on Sunday morning at the studio who was also affected by Jake's death. He was not, you know, like Jake. He was just a friend, a writer who admired Jake's art and seemed to have been sort of inspired by him. It's all so sad. Tragic, really. All these people who mourned Jake, and still do. And we never knew. We thought it was only us, that it was all about us." She fidgeted with her wedding rings as she spoke.

"Jake touched a lot of lives," Bill said softly.

Isabelle nodded, then gave the waiter her order – two scrambled eggs, toast and coffee, same as every year.

Bill ordered a western omelet, bacon and coffee. After the waiter left, he said, "I'm still so sorry I wasn't there for you, Mother, when it happened."

"Stop saying you're sorry, will you?" Isabelle said. "You're wallowing. It's long over now, and it wasn't your fault. None of it had anything to do with you."

"I should have been reachable. I shouldn't have turned off my cell."

"Why do we have to talk about this again? It's been nine months. What happened happened. I'm not blaming you for anything, and I never have."

"*I'm* blaming me, for letting you down. And for a while, when it first happened, I actually sort of blamed myself for Jake's death." Bill massaged his sore temples. "Another one of those ripple effects."

"That's ridiculous, William. Why would you blame yourself?"

"I guess partly because the whole thing was so horrible it made me kind of crazy, and I felt like the blame had to be placed somewhere, like these things don't happen for no reason. And I suppose I also blamed myself because I'm a good Catholic, Mother, and for that, I blame you." Bill smiled wanly.

"You're not making any sense," Isabelle said. She sounded so tired and exasperated.

"There was a part of me that thought the whole thing was like divine retribution for something I had done," Bill said quietly. "I know that sounds nuts. But in some weird way I continued to blame myself until I went to see Father McGowan about it, just last week...when I couldn't

135

stand dealing with it on my own anymore. He told me it was insanely egotistical to think God would do something like that to Jake as vengeance for something I had done."

"What could you possibly have done to make you believe you had earned that kind of vengeance?" Isabelle seemed curious, but also a little fearful.

"I'm sorry, Mother. I interrupted you," Bill said, shaking his head. "You were telling me about the two men you met."

"I've said all I want to say about them. Tell me what *you're* trying to say."

This was terra incognita. They didn't do this in his family, they didn't open up, and that method of operation had always served them well. Nonetheless, Bill took a deep breath and blurted it out.

"There's another woman," he said. "I was with her that night. That's why my phone was turned off." The words rushed out of his mouth as if they'd been trapped inside for too long. "I'm in love, Mother. I'm in love with someone I've known since I was a resident but lost for a long time. When I found her again two years ago it seemed like a gift from God."

"Do *not* bring God into this," Isabelle said sternly. "What about Vanessa?"

"She doesn't know. I'm sure she doesn't even suspect. We're not close enough that she'd notice."

"I didn't know you two were having problems."

"We're not; maybe that *is* the problem. Things are perfectly peaceful between us. We don't argue, we don't pick at each other....'

"So, what's wrong, William? *What's wrong?*"

"Peaceful doesn't seem like enough anymore, though before I found Larissa it was more than enough, more than most people had a right to expect. I enjoyed being married to a smart, beautiful woman, one who was a good companion and a wonderful mother. I was perfectly content. But when I found Larissa – or re-found her – I realized contentment wasn't enough."

"What's *that* supposed to mean?" Isabelle sounded angry, and Bill knew he was chipping away at the foundation of everything his mother understood and believed in, everything her life had been built around, but he couldn't stop talking.

"Just that. Companionship wasn't enough for me anymore. I had a connection with Larissa that was so strong, so amazingly profound, it made me feel like a new person. God, I can't even talk about this without using the most inane clichés."

"Why are you talking about her in the past tense?" Isabelle asked, sounding hopeful.

"After Jake's death, I pulled away from her. I felt so guilty about not being there for you that night – and for Jake – and I realized my absence was a direct result of these lies and deceptions that had taken over my life. And yes, I did honestly feel on some level like the whole thing with Jake was a big cosmic punishment. So, I tried to end it."

"Have you?"

"I tried to. I've distanced myself. I've seen her less frequently, spoken with her far less often. But I can't stop thinking about her. That's why I went to Father McGowan."

"Don't tell me he said this was all fine," Isabelle said coldly.

"No, not at all. But he did say it was ridiculous to think it had anything to do with Jake's death. The rest, he said, was up to me to figure out."

Isabelle started to take a bite of her eggs, but put the fork back down.

138

"I love you, William," she said. "You know I've always loved you and Jake more than anyone. That's never been a secret, not even from your father or Harold. But this is not something I approve of, nor is it the kind of thing I'm used to. Nothing that's happened to me in the past three days is the kind of thing I'm used to."

* * *

After getting Isabelle settled into her room at Lenox Hill, Bill walked back over to Fifth Avenue and entered the park at the 61st Street entrance. He sat down on the bench he and Larissa had for decades considered "theirs," and watched a pastel portraitist create a strikingly close likeness of a teenage girl with flowing blonde hair. He wondered when the disaffected pout that distorted the girl's beautiful features would resolve into a serenely pleasant expression. He remembered his own daughter's early teenage years. She had never been more lovely, in a fresh, soft way, and never more irritable and unhappy. It was a state of adolescent angst she outgrew by the time she was about sixteen, when she suddenly turned into a delightful young woman. Bill couldn't bring himself to think about what it would do to Marianne if he left Vanessa for Larissa.

His son was another matter altogether. Jeff would deal with it; he might even understand. For he, like Jake, was intuitive and had insight beyond his years. He might well sense his father's turmoil even now.

Bill pulled his phone out of his pocket and punched in Larissa's number.

When she answered he didn't know exactly what he wanted to say.

"You called last night," he said.

"I'm sorry. I --"

"Don't be. I've been wanting to talk to you; needing to talk to you, actually.

"I know," she said. "You told me. And it's okay. I know what you want to say, and you're right. You're absolutely right."

"Right about what?"

"We've had a good run, Bill," she said calmly. "The best of my life. But this isn't right for either one of us. It's taken me a while to figure that out, but I get it now. And I'd rather say goodbye on a good note than drag the whole thing out and risk having it all implode."

"What the hell...? Can I see you?" he said.

"I don't think that would do either of us any good, and there's no point. It's easier this way."

"Don't you love me, Larissa?"

She was silent for a long time. "Yes, I do," she said. "I love you way too much."

"So, why can't I see you?"

"Because I'm afraid we'd fall back into the old patterns that made you unhappy and guilty and me frustrated and sometimes even angry. Besides, you've made it pretty clear you're ready to end it all."

"What makes you say that?"

"Oh, come on, Bill. How can you ask that?"

"I'm sorry," he said. "You're right, I did want to. I thought I needed to. But I don't anymore. I need you."

"It's not right for either one of us," Larissa said. "You know it, I know it, and rather than continue something that's going to make both of us ultimately unhappy, I want us to keep the memories we have and move on with our lives."

"Just like that?"

"Just like that."

"What if I told you –"

"Stop it, Bill. Don't make this more painful than it is, okay? Let me keep my pride and my memories, and let me move on."

"But, what if..."

"Maybe someday," she said, "maybe when we're about a hundred, things will have changed and we'll be able to figure this out. But not now, Bill. I'm not smart enough, and I'm not strong or brave enough. Not now."

"Larissa, please."

"I have to go." She hung up.

Bill stared at the blonde teenager for a long time before flipping his phone shut.

Chapter Nine: A Huge, Perfect, and Destructive Thing

Wednesday, September 21, 2005

Frank arrived at work in time to prepare for the typically hybrid lunchtime crowd of Park Avenue charity-circuit matrons, midtown expense-account types, old fogeys who liked reliving their days as midtown expense-account types and the occasional tourist twosome who came to the Café Pierre because it was romantic and, they thought, a quintessentially New York experience. Frank hated to think the latter was really the case.

He scanned the rows of glittering bottles filled with jewel-colored liquids, checking levels and making mental notes about which ones he needed to back up with spares from the store room: Bombay Sapphire, Johnny Walker Black, Stoli, Cointreau, Pinch, Macallan 18, and Jose Cuervo. He'd also have to get Murray to replenish the Chardonnay and Pinot Noir supply, and bring up a case of Sam Adams and one of Heineken.

After completing the inventory scan, Frank began systematically wiping the bottles with a bar towel so they shone. He knew from decades of experience that fingerprints, drips, and anything else that dulled the sparkle created a small but noticeable dip in sales. People loved engaging with beautiful things, and that included sparkling bottles of colorful, crystalline liquids. That's why he always made sure his bar shelves were backed with mirrors and that the mirrors were wiped clean. Anything that enhanced the sparkle enhanced the take.

After the bottles, Frank turned his attention to stray watermarks and fingerprints on the glasses the kitchen staff had put back on the shelves early in the morning. He polished each one lovingly, rubbing hard enough to eliminate any trace of a mark but not so hard as to risk breakage. He'd seen many a fine, thin wineglass crack due to overly enthusiastic cleaning.

As he worked, his thoughts migrated to yesterday morning's visit with Larissa, an encounter he'd tried to avoid thinking about during the intervening twenty-four hours. He felt queasy remembering how he had blurted out the story of his marriage, Chloe's death, and his commemorative Tuesday morning walks in the park. He had never told anyone about those walks. It all sounded too stupid, too weak, too damn romantic. More to the point, it was private. Most people didn't even know he'd been married, and he liked it that way. He was accustomed to the persona he'd unwittingly taken on, that of the tough loner who had nothing but his job. As a matter of fact, the characterization was fairly accurate. He had nothing but his job and his memories.

Frank reached up for a dark brown bottle of Kaluha he hadn't previously paid attention to on the third shelf. He held it up to the light and tilted it to see how much liquid remained. It wasn't a drink that was called for very often these days, but when someone wanted it they really wanted it, so Frank kept it in stock. The bottle contained a good five or six shots. That'd do for now.

As he put the Kaluha back into position, he caught a glimpse of himself in the mirror. Disturbed by what he saw, he set the bottle down on the counter and took a long look at his reflection. He looked at the tiny red lines that ran through the whites of his eyes and the bags that sagged beneath them, the deep furrows in his forehead, and the rough, bulbous quality of his nose. His face reminded him of the postcard of a Rembrandt self-portrait Chloe used to keep taped to the refrigerator door. She loved that card; she said she felt moved by the profound depth and soul of the face every time she walked by it. She'd stare at it, and her lip would tremble.

She told Frank the story of how Rembrandt had lost his beloved wife Saskia at a very young age. Chloe was sure this was why the artist

145

appeared so old and weary in this portrait he painted when he was only fifty-three. When Chloe was diagnosed with leukemia she quietly removed the card from the refrigerator and never mentioned it again, but Frank found it four years later when he went through the contents of her closet. It was in a shoebox, along with two photos of Frank and the wrist corsage he had given her on their first date. They had gone dancing.

He stared hard at his image in the mirror, much as Chloe had stared at that card, and he wondered what in God's name had provoked him to tell Larissa about Chloe. He was not generally given to weaknesses of any sort. He was the bartender, after all, the stolid one. It was his job. It was also his primary means of survival. It kept him from having time to reflect, and Frank had long prided himself on never looking back, or forward for that matter.

Talking about Chloe, verbalizing his loss, had made it real. Yet, saying her name, talking about her innate sweetness and perfection, had also sort of brought her back to life. He was embarrassed he had done it and saddened by having dredged up the whole thing, but he was also left with a residual something bordering on tranquility he would never have expected, and had honestly never before experienced.

* * *

146

But that didn't make him any happier to see John Taylor walk into the Café Pierre at the height of the evening's rush hour.

Dressed in a traditional glen plaid suit and blue silk tie, John Taylor sat himself down at a round table near the window, the same one he had shared with the cute blonde a few nights ago. Like most customers, he was a creature of habit. They all seemed to gravitate to the tables or stools they'd occupied on their first visits.

He sent Murray over to take the kid's order and busied himself making some of the mixed drinks his patrons were once again requesting. Frank was happy the days of nothing-but-beer-and-wine were a thing of the past. And while he detested those frou-frou, fruity drinks and found the whole idea of a martini with anything but gin or vodka and vermouth an abomination, he liked flexing his professional muscle and producing the best damn versions of the classics in town.

He tossed a dash of bitters into an Old Fashioned and snuck another peek at John Taylor who was placing his order with Murray. Murray took the order, as usual, without saying a word then started his slow shuffle back to the bar. As he did so, John Taylor turned in Frank's direction.

He waved shyly and mouthed "hello," then pulled a small book out of his breast pocket and started reading. Thankfully, he seemed no more interested in chitchat than Frank was. Just seeing him here made Frank a little antsy, so he started mixing a Cosmopolitan on spec to have something to do. No one had ordered it, but someone would. They always did at this time of the evening. Some broad would want it sooner or later.

* * *

By the time ten o'clock rolled around, Frank had knocked back four or five Scotches, something he almost never did while on duty. He'd occasionally have a drink to keep a customer company, or if someone bought him one he'd sip at it to be polite. But tonight he had some demons to control. The kid made him think about yesterday morning, which made him think about Chloe, which was something he couldn't let himself do.

John Taylor had consumed at least three, maybe four glasses of wine. He just sat there, all alone, sipping, munching on chips and nuts, reading, and occasionally jotting something in a tiny notebook he had set on the table somewhere around drink number two. An easy enough customer, Frank thought. He didn't need help or company, didn't want to talk. He kept to himself, unlike the people who were starting to gather around the bar.

When the blowhard, tattooed fellow called Mike strolled in, Frank's fellow-feelings toward John Taylor warmed even more. He poured himself another Scotch, grabbed a glass of wine, and told Murray to man the bar.

"Name's John, right?" Frank said as he approached John Taylor's table. He put the drinks down on the table and held out his right hand.

The young man shook it and nodded. "Nice to see you."

Frank plopped himself down in the empty seat opposite John, something he would never have done, unsolicited, absent the encouragement of the drinks he'd consumed. "Where's the blonde?"

"What?"

"The lady you were with the other night," Frank said.

John pushed his empty wineglass aside and took a long sip from the one Frank had brought. "Thanks," he murmured over the rim of the glass. His dazed look told Frank the kid had had more wine than he was accustomed to. "She was my fiancée."

"Lucky man," Frank said.

"She *was* my fiancée," John said. "It's over."

"I'm sorry," Frank said, taking a chance on the obvious response.

"Me too," John said, "in a way."

Poor guy seemed pretty much at sea.

"I think I might have loved her." He paused, breathed deeply, took a drink and swallowed hard. "She's a good person...much better than I am. And I kind of liked knowing what was going to be happening in my life. Now I have no idea."

"Why'd she leave?" Frank said, his bartender skills kicking in. He recognized a man who needed to talk.

"She didn't," John said. "I did."

"Why?"

"It wasn't right between us. She didn't know who I was, what I needed. Or if she did, she tried to pretend it wasn't real. I knew that if I leveled with her, forced her to see what I'm all about, forced her to understand, she'd be gone. So, I took a shortcut and left, so she wouldn't have to."

"That's tough, kid," Frank said. "How'd she take it?"

"Too well," John said wryly. "The thing she was most upset about was how her parents would take it - you know, after all their preparations."

Before Frank could respond, he saw Isabelle Peretti walk into the Café. How odd to see her here twice in one week. She spotted him, and headed in his direction.

She looked like a million bucks, dressed in a bright green knit suit with shiny brass buttons, hair pulled back just so, as always. But she seemed odd; she reeled from side to side as she walked. "Here, have a seat." He held the back rim of the faux-French upholstered chair he'd been sitting in while she lowered herself carefully into it.

"I remember you; you're Jake's neighbor," she said to John.

"Yes," he said, holding out his hand, "John Taylor." Frank could see the young man was too worn out to stand.

Isabelle took his hand and held onto it.

"I didn't know you two knew each other," she said.

"We don't really," Frank said. "We met yesterday at a mutual friend's house." That was enough said; Mrs. P wasn't the kind of woman you engaged in extraneous conversation. "What can I get you to drink?"

"A Brandy Alexander," she said with confidence. "You made me a very nice one the other night."

"Coming right up," he said, and went to the bar to mix a quick one and make sure Murray had things under control. When he got back to the

151

table, he set the Brandy Alexander in front of Mrs. P and another wine in front of John. "On the house."

"Now tell me," he said, dragging a chair for himself over from a neighboring table and settling comfortably back into his bartender role, "how do you two know each other?"

"We met at my grandson's studio," Isabelle said. "Mr. Taylor has a studio across the hall. He's a writer, you know."

"No, I didn't," Frank said. "Thought you were a lawyer."

"I am," John said. "Mrs. Peretti's being generous. I write short stories, but I haven't had any published."

"And you knew Jake?" Frank said to John.

"I don't want to talk about him," Isabelle said abruptly.

"Sorry," Frank said. "I didn't mean to...."

"I met the man I told you about," Isabelle said to Frank, "the one who broke into Jake's studio and almost died."

"Yeah? How'd *that* happen?"

"I visited him in the hospital," she said, and took a sip of her drink.

"Did you find out what it was all about?" Frank said. "Why he broke in and did what he did there?"

"Love," she murmured.

"What?"

"He was in love with my grandson."

"I don't understand how that – "

"Love can be destructive." She made the pronouncement with the gravitas of the pope issuing an encyclical. "It nearly destroyed that man." She took a long drink. Frank signaled Murray for another, taking a chance Murray might figure out how to make it. "And it might destroy my son's marriage."

"*Love* might?" Frank was now utterly baffled.

Isabelle nodded. "It's very powerful. Hugely powerful. And sometimes apparently uncontrollable. After almost eighty years of living on this earth, I'm just now finding that out."

"That's why I came back here to see you," she said to Frank. "I want to talk about this, and it's not the kind of thing my friends talk about. We don't really talk." She slurred her words, and she'd hardly had half a drink.

"Look at those people," she said, nodding toward a middle-aged couple at a nearby table. Frank recognized the petite woman and broad-shouldered man as a twosome who came in every few months, usually around closing time. Innocuous enough. He figured them to be out-of-towners. They'd have a couple of nightcaps and quiet laughs, and be on their way.

"Look at the way they admire each other," Isabelle said dreamily, "and the way they touch each other. Look...he's holding her hand. Look at how she touches his face...reverently. And how gently he pulls her head over to kiss her on the mouth. Look at the way they laugh, and the way they seem to have so much to say to each other they can't stop talking." Isabelle took a deep breath. "The two of them make a whole world; they don't need an entourage. They're like teenagers, the way they cling to one another. They can't get enough of each other. I believe that's love. I don't know if it's right or wrong, but it's very, very powerful."

The man handed the woman a small white box with a purple satin ribbon on it. She pulled the ribbon off and tied it around his wrist before opening the box.

"But why do you say it's destructive?" Frank asked.

"I think real love is organic," she said. "And even a thousand years ago when I took science we learned that organic things either grow or die. If it's not killed, it can grow and evolve into a perfect thing, or so they say, but to do so it might tear down anything that gets in its way." She paused. "That's what I've learned over these past few days."

"Is it worth it?" John asked.

"I'm not sure," Isabelle said, as if she'd considered that very question. "I've never experienced that kind of love myself, not in a romantic way. I did have a very powerful love for Jake, but that's different. I never had it for my husband. We cared deeply for each other and we were devoted to each other from the day we met until the day he died. We certainly had great affection for each other, but we didn't have that powerful thing that drew us inexorably together, the thing Shakespeare talks about in his sonnets, not like those two...or like my son and his girlfriend...or like the thing the man named Phillip apparently had for my grandson.

"What Carter and I had was not such a consuming kind of affection, but that was all right." She touched the large diamond solitaire flanked by two baguettes which she wore on her left ring finger, and turned it around and around as she spoke. "What we had made us both terribly content, though I now wonder if that's the same thing as being happy. I wonder if I missed something. My son recently referred to his perfectly content relationship with his perfectly lovely wife as 'going through the motions.' Said he didn't know there was anything more, until his old friend came back into his life. That's when the irresistible, powerful thing took over. The beautiful, amazing and destructive thing. Ironic, isn't it?" She turned to John Taylor. "What about you and your fiancée?"

"I've left her," John said quietly.

"Good," Isabelle said without hesitation. She touched his arm lightly. "One mustn't go into a marriage with doubts. I've always known that. But what I also believe now is that one should never, ever enter into a marriage that lacks that special passion I'm just now finding out about, that potentially destructive edge that has the capacity to render each person uniquely and ideally complete.

"I'm coming to believe that maybe there's nothing in the world more important, no force on earth so great, and that not to experience it would be to miss one of the biggest things life has to offer. No matter how many wonderful things you do or places you go, you could end up living a small life." Her voice trailed off.

Frank wondered if his perfect love for Chloe might have been destructive, if it might have rendered his subsequent life small.

"Love doesn't *have* to be destructive," Isabelle said, as if responding to his thoughts. "It need not even be terribly dramatic. If only the people who were meant to be together *could* be together, there would be nothing less destructive or more constructive and productive in the world. That's what I'm thinking. It's not a Catholic thought, God knows, but it's what I'm thinking."

Isabelle gulped her drink, and pushed away the second one Murray had brought over.

"You've obviously thought a lot about this," Frank said.

"I've had some time." She pulled up her green sleeve to reveal a plastic hospital I.D. bracelet. "I've been in the hospital."

"Why?" Frank said. "You okay?"

"It was just a physical, but they found a small lump yesterday and took a biopsy early this morning. Maybe the anesthetizing drugs made me think – they're certainly making me talk," she said. "Or maybe it was the little brush up against the notion of mortality that brought on all this uncharacteristic reflection. And all this ridiculous chatter. Sorry, I just keep going on.... Maybe it's the realization that I'm past the point where I can make up for things I missed. I don't know. But after my son brought me back here from Lenox Hill it all started to come together." She turned to John. "Don't miss the things I missed. Wait until it's true and right...and gigantic and powerful."

She turned to Frank. "Have you felt this?"

He nodded.

"Good. Hold onto it." Isabelle's face flushed, her head dropped, and her eyes rolled up a little in their sockets. "Please forgive my babbling," she whispered. "They told me not to drink this evening. Something about the drugs."

"Is your son still here?" Frank asked, becoming concerned.

"No," she said. "I insisted he go home. I told him I needed to rest."

Chapter Ten: I Can't Do This Anymore

Saturday, September 24, 2005

Bill heard her voice as soon as he walked into the foyer outside the Café Carlyle.   It was as clear and resonant as it had been the first time he'd heard it at that rattrap motel in Jersey City. But sadder. Bill was sure he heard notes of melancholy; he had to believe she missed him as much as he did her.

As soon as the singing stopped it was replaced by sustained applause peppered with a few whistles and cheers, then came the opening strains of Larissa's signature closing number, "In Between Goodbyes." The audience fell silent, and the ensemble of piano, sax and bass suspended its playing after the first few notes, leaving that ethereal voice out there on its own.

When Larissa wrapped the number up, the room exploded with applause. Through the closed glass door, Bill saw the audience rise to it collective feet. Some whistled, some shouted, some even stomped. He had tried to make a reservation for the performance but the month's run was fully booked and the waiting list was twenty-three parties deep.

At times like this, the idea that such a beautiful, talented, and beloved woman could ever have had the least bit of interest in him seemed ludicrous. The futility, even absurdity, of his plan to intercept her as she exited, insist that she talk with him, and thereby win her back, became clear. He nodded to the coat-check woman who had been keeping a somewhat suspicious watch on him, and walked out onto Madison Avenue.

For the past few days, ever since their last phone conversation, Larissa had refused to speak with him. He had left messages – at least four or five – enough that he recognized leaving more would be a vain effort, which was why he was here.

But being privy to the effusive affection heaped upon her by these strangers, he realized he was just one more in a long line of admirers. The thought made him feel ridiculous, like a groupie begging for attention. He leaned against the cold building wall and took a deep breath of evening air. For the first time in decades, he craved a cigarette.

As dozens of people walked out of the Café Carlyle, chattering brightly about how wonderful the show had been, Bill spotted a few stars in the blue-black sky, a rare sighting in New York. Then he saw a large, clear moon illuminating the quiet corridor Madison Avenue becomes at night. He thought about the wooden box in the shape of a quarter moon Larissa

160

had given him a year ago. She had told him to remember, every night, that no matter where they each were they were sharing the same moon, and that it would somehow form a link between them.

The crowd dwindled to nothing, and Bill stood under the night sky until he smelled a familiar scent. Calycanthus, a perfume he had brought Larissa from Venice. He turned to see a tall woman in a red fox coat step into a waiting cab.

"Larissa," he shouted as she was about to close the door.

She turned in his direction, and didn't look pleased.

He walked to the curb and leaned into the cab's open door. "Can we go somewhere and talk?"

She hesitated, then apologized to the cabbie, handed him a ten-dollar bill, and stepped out.

"What's there to talk about?" she said as the cab drove off.

"Please, let me walk you across the park," he said.

* * *

It was dark and quiet at Picholine, just as it had been the first time Bill had brought her here, two years ago, the night after they had become reacquainted at Bemelman's.

Larissa had surprised him with a dinner here on the first anniversary of that reuniting, a date it would never have occurred to Bill to take note of. They had come again on Larissa's birthday, and thus it had become their favorite special occasion restaurant. She liked to think of the cozy, romantic hideaway as "our place." It made her happy, she said, in a world that was of necessity divided into things that were "yours" and "mine" to have a place that was "ours." Bill had chuckled at the notion, pretending to be amused, but in fact was deeply touched.

Picholine had seemed the perfect place for tonight, and Bill had optimistically reserved "our table," hoping Larissa would actually come with him. And now here they were, sharing the banquette, as always. The only difference was that Larissa's leg was not rubbing up against his, as it usually did. That and the uncomfortable silence that hung between them.

After the waiter poured two glasses of Veuve Clicquot, Bill raised his in Larissa's direction. "Thank you for coming with me." They touched glasses. "I love you, Larissa. I have since I met you, and I always will. I want to be with you." He nervously took a sip of champagne.

Larissa set her glass back down on the table without taking a drink.

"What are you thinking?" he asked.

"I guess I'm wondering what you mean by that."

"By what?"

"Wanting to be with me. In view of everything we've been through, I have no idea what that means."

"It means I want to spend my life with you."

"Like we have, you mean? Spend time together whenever you can get into the city?"

"No. I mean I want you to be there when I go to bed at night and when I wake up in the morning. And I want you to be there in between."

"What about... I mean...that's hardly realistic, Bill."

He didn't know what to say.

"You've always made the limits of our relationship clear," she said, "even without exactly stating them. There were no false representations, no pretensions. You were happy to have what we had, and so was I...for a while." She picked up her glass and took a small sip. "But I can't do this anymore. It's not me, and it's making me crazy." She blew out the votive candle on the table and watched a wisp of gray smoke rise. "Remember that movie, the one about the gay cowboys?"

"*Brokeback Mountain,*" he said. He was used to filling in the blanks; she never remembered the names of movies or their characters.

"Right," she said. "Remember how the one cowboy was able to carry on the covert same-time-next-year kind of love affair and still live a pretty decent life back home, and how the other couldn't do it? How the one character had a way of compartmentalizing his relationships so they could peacefully coexist, while the other was so consumed by his lover that the relationship bled into his whole life and he lost everything, including his sanity?"

Bill nodded, afraid of what was coming next.

"I'm the second cowboy," she said. "I've learned that I can't do the covert thing...or the halfway thing. I can't live with a tiny piece of the man I love. I can't live a life where I have to hide the thing that's most important to me. And I can't keep deceiving the people I care about."

"I've loved you for a long time, Bill, but I can't do this. For two years, I believed I could, but not anymore. It isn't working. It's screwing up my sense of who I am and where I belong in the world. At first it filled me up, but now it's leaving me with a huge emptiness."

She took a sip of champagne. "I wasn't the one who was supposed to be doing the talking tonight, was I?"

* * *

"My mother was diagnosed with cancer a few days ago," Bill said. "I thought she was going to die."

"Oh, my God," Larissa said. "I'm so sorry." She touched his hand gently.

Bill waited for the waiter to pick up their practically untouched appetizers and serve their entrees before continuing.

"It's okay. It was a misdiagnosis. She had a biopsy – breast lump – a few days ago, and I got the lab to expedite the results. Professional courtesy. Her doctor told me the next day she had a particularly virulent form of cancer that was highly likely to have metastasized." Bill picked up his fork and poked at his rack of lamb. "I spoke with a surgeon friend at Sloan-Kettering. He said he wouldn't recommend operating. It wouldn't do any good, and at her age the risks would outweigh the benefits. He said we should concentrate our efforts on keeping her comfortable. I hate that phrase."

"But they were wrong? They screwed up?" Larissa said.

Bill nodded. "Screwed up big. I suppose it's my fault for pushing them to expedite, but the lab called back yesterday and said they had gotten two biopsies switched. Hers was fine. Benign nodule. Nothing..." he said.

"But, Jesus, I keep thinking about the woman who's going to get the bullet my mother dodged."

"Why are you telling me this?" Larissa said.

"Because it made everything more urgent. One day, my mother was fine; the next, we were planning her funeral, for God's sake. She was talking to her lawyer about her will. She was deciding how she wanted to spend her final days. It was one of those wakeup calls, one of those things that reminds you life is fragile and fleeting, and that anything you might want to do on this earth you'd better do. You know?"

Larissa fingered her glass nervously.

"I want to be with you," he said. "That's what I want to do on this earth more than anything else."

* * *

Early in their re-acquaintanceship, Bill had taken Larissa to the Metropolitan Museum of Art for a Friday evening concert. They had arrived early and strolled the Italian Renaissance galleries, studying elegant religious images created by Raphael, Botticelli, Lippi and Angelico. Bill had enjoyed sharing his knowledge of art with her, telling her stories of the times, the artists, the subjects and the patrons. He knew she would enjoy the gold leaf detailing, the brilliant colors, and the beautiful subjects. At the end of his discourse he asked her which of the works was her favorite.

"It's not here," she said. "It's downstairs."

He was surprised to learn she was sufficiently familiar with the museum to have a favorite all her own. "Will you take me to see it?"

With the assurance of one who had traveled the serpentine route many times, Larissa took him downstairs to the School of Paris galleries and stopped in front of Picasso's portrait of Gertrude Stein. A massive, somber mountain of a presence with a face resembling an angular mask, Gertrude was hardly an icon of great beauty, and her portrait was frankly not a painting Bill would have paid any attention to.

"Why is this your favorite?" he asked.

"I love her story," Larissa said. "I don't pretend to understand most of her writing, but I love the crazy energy of her life, and I think this picture captures the essence of who she was. It's tough and strong and nonconformist, but there's a tiny bit of gentleness and even gentility in her expression and in the soft easiness of her hands." Larissa blushed. "I just like it."

That's when Bill realized there was a great deal he didn't know about Larissa, and he looked forward to peeling away the layers.

And indeed, the more he learned about her the more he loved her. He found her combination of worldliness and naiveté, strength and vulnerability, confidence and insecurity, to be challenging, sweet, always interesting, and often surprising. Not only did she love Gertrude Stein, she was crazy for Danielle Steel. She loved handicapping horse races, adored the Berlin Philharmonic, had a box at the Metropolitan Opera, and box seats for the Mets. The same woman who once drove all the way to Indiana for a banana milkshake at Steak 'n Shake bought dozens of Hermes scarves because she thought they were among the most beautiful things on earth. But she never wore them because she was afraid she'd mess them up.

He knew life with Larissa would be an endless adventure.

* * *

As the waiter rolled the formidable cheese cart up to their table, Bill heard a familiar voice call his name, and looked up to see his Greenwich neighbors, Joe and Angela Calhoun.

"What the hell are you doing here, buddy?" Joe said, slapping him on the shoulder.

168

"Hey, Joe, good to see you." Bill stood up and tried to act casual as he took Joe's hand, but his heart was racing. "Angela, you look fabulous, as always." He gave her a peck on the cheek.

"Where's Vanessa?" she asked, pointedly. Angela and Vanessa were great friends, and compatriots on the suburban charity circuit.

"She's home," he said. "I've been at one of the world's most boring urology conferences. It's so bad that my colleague," he gestured toward Larissa, "and I finally skipped out on the rubber chicken and endless speeches to get some peace and quiet and real food."

Angela nodded but didn't look convinced. Bill knew Larissa looked more like a lounge singer than a physician, and he knew the details of this evening would get back to Vanessa.

"Good for you for making the escape, pal," Joe said with a big thumbs-up. "Hope your meal was as good as ours. I had the venison and Angie had the salmon. Both terrific." Then he tipped an imaginary hat. "We've got to run. Catching the train back to Greenwich."

"Are you driving back tonight?" Angela said to Bill.

"Yeah," Bill said. "Want a lift?"

"No, thanks," Joe said. "We're good." He winked at Bill and took Angela's arm. "See you at the club on Monday night?"

169

"Wouldn't miss it," Bill said.

Then they were gone.

Bill waved off the waiter, saying they would pass on the cheese course. Larissa stared at the tablecloth.

"I'm sorry," he said. "I didn't know what to say."

She didn't speak.

"I panicked," he said.

Larissa bit her lip and pushed a hank of hair behind her ear.

"I'm sorry," Bill repeated.

"So am I."

Chapter Eleven: A Life's Work

Saturday, September 24, 2005

Mike looked her over, head to toe. The packaging was pretty
decent: broad hips poured into a short black skirt; long legs encased in
flashy silver fishnet; thick blonde hair he could really grab onto; and a shelf
practically out to the street – silicone for sure, but who cared? She even
had pleasant features, a face that might have been beautiful if it hadn't been
so weathered and so damn hard. She couldn't have been older than mid-
thirties but looked like she'd seen a lot more of the world than anyone
should. Mike liked that. He appreciated education, and liked the idea that
a hooker could teach him something.

He nodded in her direction and pulled out his wallet.

"Two hundred," she said in a calm voice that neither begged for
nor rejected the offer implicit in his gesture.

"Kind of high, don't you think?"

She took a drag on her cigarette and blew a leisurely smoke ring.
"You get what you pay for." She delivered the line in a manner that
suggested she repeated it too many times a day. "Take it or leave it."

Mike liked feisty, and he liked a challenge. "What do I get for that?" he asked with a leer.

"Standard," she replied. "Four-fifty and you can have whatever you want."

"I think standard will hold me. Do you take credit?"

"Very funny," she said wearily, "but you're not paying me enough to laugh. Give me $450 and I'll chuckle at anything you want."

Mike reached into his pocket, pulled out a wad of bills and peeled off two hundreds.

She hadn't made eye contact with him since her initial come-on, and wasn't cooperating now. She'd been looking mostly across the street, though occasionally her glance would fall onto a putrid yellow puddle on the pavement near his feet. Mike wondered if she was doing business with a pimp over there in the shadowy alley off Eighth Avenue, or if this was just the way she was, the way it would be all evening. He hoped it was the former, because her remoteness kind of freaked him out. It's not like he was after a soul mate, but he liked some eye contact when he talked, and it kind of pissed him off when he didn't get it.

To make the point, he grabbed her chin and turned her face toward him, enjoying the way the dragon tattoo on the back of his hand glowed in the halogen street lighting against her powdery pale face. "I'm paying you enough to look at me, babe."

"My name's Lola," she said, "not babe. And actually, you're not."

* * *

Mike's preferred locale for liaisons, as he liked to think of meetings like this, was the Hotel Chelsea on 23rd. Considering himself a bit of a connoisseur of both art and literature, he liked the sense of history here: the third-rate paintings by one-time first-rate artists that still decorated the public areas. He also liked knowing that Mark Twain, O. Henry, Thomas Wolfe, Dylan Thomas, William Burroughs, and even Edgar Lee Masters, for God's sake, had spent time here. When he was stoned enough, he could actually feel the spirits of Larry Rivers and the Warhol coven drifting through the hallways.

That the place was kind of off-putting in its décor, kind of seedy in its upkeep, and downright bizarre in its current-day clientele made it all the more appealing. When Mike was with someone like Lola, he didn't want to be at the Goddamn Ritz, or the Pierre, not that he'd ever actually been in a room there. He wanted a place like this. It felt right.

He walked up to the check-in counter, proud to be seen with someone as striking as Lola, and asked for room 327, his favorite. Then, indulging his lifelong fear of elevators, he pointed Lola to the stairs and followed her up, admiring the way her calf muscles contracted and bulged with each step. They reminded him of his own biceps, which happened to be his favorite part of his body.

He unlocked the door to 327 and allowed Lola to precede him in, but he wouldn't let her turn on the lights. He preferred having the cheesy neon glow of 23rd Street illuminate the room. It made him feel like he was in an Edward Hopper painting, and that gave him a vague sense of importance. Maybe that was too strong a word. Maybe it just made him feel connected to something in the mainstream flow of human existence that he normally didn't.

* * *

Though it was a habit he had long since shed, Mike had once been a voracious reader. While his three older brothers were wrestling, swimming, shooting hoops, lobbing tennis balls, swinging polo mallets, driving golf balls, sailing, playing football, and hitting on anything female, Mike was mostly sitting in the mahogany-paneled den in Winnetka or on the wide veranda at the back of the summer house in Lake Geneva with a book in his hand.

He read enormous tomes of history and biography; he loved art books filled with pictures of luscious nudes, fertile landscapes, horses, and lavish, fruit-filled still lifes; he devoured animal stories and tales of adventure; and he went through mystery novels so quickly his mother once quipped that his reading habit would bankrupt the family. He generally preferred living life vicariously through his books to moving out of the den or off the veranda and living it in person.

So, Mike became a little soft, physically and maybe emotionally too. While his brothers grew bigger, louder and ever more virile, he became rounder, quieter, and more and more engaged in his various worlds of the mind.

It was all right. No one bothered him too much about it. His father was happy to have three sons who shared his own interests – which ran to sports and women – and simply didn't take much notice of the fourth. His mother rather enjoyed Mike's company when she had time, and occasionally engaged him in conversations about what he was reading. His eldest two brothers generally ignored him in a way that was neither good nor bad. They happened to live in the same house and managed to mostly stay out of his way, as he stayed out of theirs, and that was that. No harm, no foul, as they would have put it. It was only rarely that they would tease him, and then he could find release in capturing small animals, like squirrels or chipmunks, and tormenting them as he felt he was being tormented. That usually took care of the pain.

But it was different with his youngest brother, Chad. Though he was every bit the tough guy the older ones were, Chad seemed to genuinely enjoy being around Mike, though Mike never understood why. Maybe it stemmed from the proximity in age, but he seemed to like sitting with Mike, talking about whatever...ordinary stuff. Often not talking at all. Sometimes, they would look for images in clouds or for constellations at night; other times, they would watch old movies or sitcom reruns on TV. Once in a while, they would hang out in a boat on the lake.

Chad was not only Mike's best friend, he was his only friend. But that was okay. He was exactly enough.

* * *

Lola settled herself onto the bed and lit a cigarette. After inhaling deeply, she held the pack out to Mike.

"No thanks," he said.

She put her black-stiletto-clad feet up on the bed, crossed her legs, and leaned back against the worn red cloth headboard, one arm behind her head. She tipped the ash from her cigarette into her hand and blew it off onto the shag rug. "So? Are you ready?"

Mike sat down at the foot of the bed and kicked off his shoes.

"How'd you get into this line of work?" he asked.

"Why? You need a job?"

"I'm serious. I want to know about you." He put a hand on her leg and ran it up and down, feeling the rough fishnet against his palm. He ran his hand up to where the fishnet ended and found the garters. With a practiced gesture, he snapped open one, then the other, and pulled the stocking down to her ankle, just above the strap of her shoe. He turned slightly and did the same with the other, then examined Lola's bare legs.

"Nice," he said. "So, what was the career path?"

"Do you want to do it or not?" Lola said. "You didn't pay for all night."

"I want to talk," Mike said.

"Jesus," Lola mumbled, and took another drag on her cigarette, this one so deep and long it made her cough.

"You should give that crap up," Mike said. "Try drinking instead."

"Both works for me," Lola replied, "as long as there are a few drugs thrown in."

"How'd you get started?"

"We're not pals, and I'm not going to talk about this."

"Then tell me how you like it when you do it. What's it like with guys like me? Is it fun? Is it heady? Is it satisfying? Is it love?"

"It's none of the first three things, and I have no idea what love is," she said, "but I'm pretty damn sure it has nothing to do with this business." She crushed the butt of her cigarette out in her calloused hand and dropped it onto the bedspread. "What's *with* you, anyway?"

"Me neither," he said, ignoring the question. "I don't know about love either. Tell you the truth, I don't think it exists. I think it's a phony construct."

"Why are we doing this? Why are we talking? I told you up front I didn't want to be your friend."

"I know. I'm not asking for that. I just want to sit here with you...and touch you a little...and talk."

"It's your dime, pal, but I don't have all night. I have an hour."

"That's fine. I just want to tell you one thing."

"So, tell me and get it over with."

Lola was obviously bored, which annoyed Mike, so he said what he wanted to say. No prelude, no explanation.

"I killed a guy."

She snapped to attention and looked at him full-on for the first time.

"Why are you telling me this?"

"I want to talk about it, and you're here."

* * *

Mike loved summertime, when the family would leave Winnetka and head for Lake Geneva. His father was only there on weekends, but he, his mother and his brothers would have three glorious months – just about forever – to hang out and do pretty much whatever they wanted. But the year Mike turned twelve, the pattern changed abruptly.

Chad had come home from school one day in June, accompanied by his father. His blue uniform was rumpled, he was shaky, actually trembling, and he was totally silent. His father pushed him toward the stairs and told him to go to his room.

Mike followed his brother upstairs. "What's wrong with you? Why's Dad home from work so early? And why'd he bring you home from school?"

Chad went into his room and shut the door.

Mike turned to find his mother behind him. "Daddy and Chad are going up to Lake Geneva for a day or two. There's something they need to talk about."

Mike would never forget the way Chad looked at him as he left for Wisconsin that evening. It was as if he was numb, like he didn't know what to say and wouldn't have been capable of saying it if he had. That was the last time Mike saw him.

* * *

"Why are you so spooked?" Mike asked Lola, who had pulled her stockings back up, and snapped them into their garters.

"I'm not spooked," she said with a tremble in her voice. "Here." She tossed the two hundred-dollar bills onto the bed. "I gotta get going."

She tried to get up but Mike grabbed her thin arm with his muscular one, and was pleased to notice she was now making sustained eye contact with him. He took the two bills and stuffed them down the front of her camisole, enjoying the feel of her firm implants. "My hour's not up, and I'm not done talking."

He shoved her back onto the bed, and she regained a small measure of the moxie that had originally attracted him. "Okay, so talk and get it over with," she said. But her expression belied the snappy tone of her voice.

"Like I said, I killed a guy. That's what I want to talk about."

She chewed the left side of her lower lip so hard she got bright red lipstick on the corner of her front tooth. Her discomfort pleased Mike. She recoiled as he wiped her tooth off with his finger.

"See, my brother died when I was little. I killed this guy as retribution."

"Did the guy kill your brother?"

"No," Mike said, "but the guy's flaming fag lover might as well have killed him. He messed with my brother when he was a kid, and my brother died because of it. Might have been an accident, might have been suicide, might have been my old man killed him so he wouldn't have to live with a fag boy. No one knows for sure. Only sure thing is it wouldn't have happened if Phil-the-fag hadn't messed with him."

"So, why didn't you kill this guy Phil?"

"I thought about it, but figured that would let him off too easy. He killed the only person I ever cared about, so I decided to kill the one he cared about. Seemed neat. Symmetrical."

And with that Mike began once again telling the story of the night in Central Park when he killed Jake. It was maybe the tenth time he'd told it, and each time had been right in this room to a girl very much like Lola.

He wasn't sure why he needed to tell the story over and over. It was partly that he wanted them all to say he'd done the right thing, the only thing he could have done. The fag named Phil had taken away his only friend, and rendered his mother so remote she was virtually absent for the rest of her short life; the fag obviously needed to be taught a lesson. Mike insisted that all his listeners agree with him on that – that this was merely justice being meted out – and they always did. He knew it was probably because they were terrified, rather than because they meant it, but the validation still felt good.

He also repeated the story over and over because he was curious to see how many times he could tell it before someone caught up with him. It seemed odd that he'd told like half the whores in Chelsea, and here he was, still out and about, walking the streets a free man.

* * *

Mike didn't read much after Chad's death. At first, it was a matter of concentration. The fact of the matter was he wanted nothing more than to lose himself in the plot of an adventure story or the life of an American

182

hero or in a book filled with beautiful pictures, but when it was quiet and he would open the pages of one of his favorite books the only thing he could see was Chad, and the only thing he could feel was sadness. He couldn't concentrate from one page to the next.

One day, he gave his mother a book of poems in the hope that their music and messages might bring her out of her fog and back to herself, and she thanked him. She kissed the top of his head, told him he was a good boy for attending to her, and stuck the book on a shelf in the den in Winnetka, where it stayed until the house was sold.

So books, he learned, were not the answer.

Torturing animals didn't work either. It seemed such a small and insignificant thing to do, relative to what had happened to Chad. The only thing that made Mike temporarily forget his dead brother was sweat. He found that when he pumped iron, ran for miles, tackled his brothers in a football game, duked it out with other boys on a wrestling mat, or whacked the hell out of a baseball, his mind would go virtually blank. He could release some of the sadness and anger, and almost cope. But if he stopped to think, it was all over. So he pumped and tackled and punched and whacked his way through middle school and prep school, then made the cut for a semipro baseball team in Elizabeth, New Jersey.

For the three years he was on the team he was admired for his handsome good looks and his strength and athleticism; he had bulked up astonishingly since he stopped reading. He had grown vertically, as well, topping off at around six foot four. He was widely admired for the many tattoos he had gotten in the hope that their heat would sear some of the pain out of him. But it hadn't.

Mike also became known for his very short fuse. As he grew bigger and more powerful, more physical and less cerebral, he became used to having his way and angered easily when he didn't get it. A nearly fatal swing at an ump who made a bad call ended his baseball career.

His coach, who knew Mike's story and genuinely liked him, told him he'd pay for Mike to see a shrink. Said it would save his life. Hard to say, maybe it had. The meds calmed him down enough to move into Manhattan on his own, where he took a few bit parts in commercials and even did a little work as a personal trainer, but that was never right. He was no good at one-on-one. He lived mostly off the money his brothers sent him from Chicago, until his Dad died and left him pretty well set on his own.

It was, in fact, it was his Dad's death that made Mike decide life was short and he needed to get off the meds that had been zapping the pizzazz out of him for all these years. It was time, he figured, to get his own life back...whatever that might be. Within weeks of liberating his body from the stranglehold of the drugs, his mission became crystal clear. It was up to him to avenge Chad's death. It was so obvious, and so good to have a reason to live.

That he found Phil Maxwell so easily, and that the man lived right here in Manhattan, Mike took as the clearest of messages from whatever messengers God or destiny might employ that he had indeed discovered his mission.

* * *

After he finished telling Lola the story of that night in Central Park, she stood up cautiously. "Can I go now?"

"If that's what you'd like," he said.

"Want your money back?" she said.

"No, hold onto it, babe." He loved being magnanimous; that's probably why he was still walking the streets, instead of behind bars. "As they say, you've got nothing to sell but your time."

"You don't like sex?" she said.

"I can take it or leave it."

Lola pulled her tight black skirt down and smoothed it with her hands. "You're an unusual guy." She flung her blonde hair off her face with a toss of her head. "And you've got quite a story."

Mike grabbed her by the hair and pulled hard, then he yanked her arm and jerked her back down onto the bed. He put his face right up against hers and watched her fear grow. "Are you saying you don't believe me?"

She shook her head. "No, no..... I was only saying...."

"You said I had 'quite a *story*.' Makes it sound like a lie.'"

"No... I didn't mean... No, I believe you."

He shoved her so hard she ended up sprawled on the bed with her hair flared out around her head like an aura. "Every fucking word of what I told you is the truth. Every one."

"I believe you. Jesus Christ, I promise I believe you."

Chapter Twelve: There Are Some Things You Can't Do In Eternity

Saturday, September 24, 2005

"There's something different about you, Isabelle," Father McGuire said, "something I can't quite put my finger on." He leaned slightly forward as he spoke, resting his elbows on the worn upholstery of the faded red armchair he always occupied when he and Isabelle conferred in his office at St. Patrick's. "It's a sort of softness."

"Softness?" she said. It wasn't a term she had ever associated with herself and she had no idea what he meant. Besides, she had only been in Father McGuire's office for ten minutes and they'd done nothing but exchange pleasantries.

"Maybe that's not the right word," he said quietly. "You just seem a little more open than usual."

"I don't know what you mean by that, Father." As she spoke, she focused on the carved linden wood crucifix that hung on the wall over his head. "I certainly don't feel soft...or open." She could feel her facial muscles tense even as she spoke the words.

"Vulnerable?" he said. "Do you feel vulnerable?"

187

She thought before responding. "Yes, I suppose I do."

"I think that's what I'm seeing," he said, scrutinizing her face in a way that made her shift uncomfortably in her chair. "You've always been very guarded, very careful, and completely in charge of yourself and your surroundings, in charge of what you would let in and what you would keep out. That showed in your bearing and in your face, and of course in what you've always said. But you look and seem more human now, Isabelle, as if maybe you don't have all the answers. You look more like the rest of us feel, and I'm delighted by that."

"Why would you say that?"

"There's a lot out there, Isabelle, a lot you miss by filtering the world and preemptively defending yourself. There are difficult and hurtful things, to be sure, which is why we all feel vulnerable at times, but there are fulfilling things too, things you can only experience while you're here on earth, things eternity doesn't offer. You have the means and emotional strength to take it all in. To be honest, I've long felt it was a shame you couldn't allow yourself to."

Isabelle didn't know what to make of the words of this priest she'd known for decades. "You've never said anything about this before," she said.

"It never occurred to me that you might be able to hear it, or that you might change this way," he said with a hint of a smile. "Forgive me for going on. What did you want to talk about?"

Father McGuire's hair had long ago turned silver and his face was ruddy, mottled and wrinkled, but she noticed his eyes were as clear as ever. She took a deep breath, and started talking. "For the first time in my life, I'm doubting my faith," she said. "When Carter died, my faith was my salvation, at least playing out the rituals was. It gave me direction, diversion, and a measure of comfort. *You* gave me comfort. When Jake died, even though I knew he never felt entirely comfortable in the Church, I turned to you again...you and the ritual and the institution. And it got me through that terrible time.

"But now I'm encountering people and things that seem good and right and perhaps even part of some divine plan, and they're living lives that are anathema to the teachings of the church." She thought about Phillip's love for another man and William's for a woman who was not his wife. "I'm meeting people for whom the church should be finding answers, but it isn't." She thought about the man named Sam who lived outside Jake's building, and young John Taylor, alone and at sea. "I don't know where it all leaves me, Father." She looked at the crucifix again.

Father McGuire leaned over and touched Isabelle's hand as if it were a precious, fragile thing. "You're questioning, Isabelle. For the first time in your life you're questioning the foundations of your faith." He spoke gently. "That's healthy, because when you figure it out – when you find out what your faith really means to you – it will be stronger than ever, and more sustaining.

"And the vulnerability you're feeling, that's just what life's all about when you open yourself up to the world. Nothing's truly safe, nothing's absolutely predictable or clear...not even your faith. It's scary when you first recognize that this is the nature of the world, and even more frightening when you realize that, no matter how many people and walls and reinforcements you surround yourself with, in the end you're all you've really got. It's terrifying at times, but also liberating. No one can control you, stop you, stand in your way, or tell you what to do. Ultimately, no one. Not only *must* you negotiate your way through the world by yourself, you *can*."

Isabelle felt queasy and began to wish she had not come to see Father McGuire. In the past, her visits with him had been comforting, reassuring. They had talked of God, of Jesus, of divine love and sacrifice, of philanthropy and good deeds, of a life well lived and assurances of

190

eternity. They had talked, too often, of death and the hereafter, of surviving loss and carrying on, and of the peace inherent in surrendering to powers greater than oneself. But this talk today left her hanging, dangling on her own in a strange, foreign place filled with people who acted differently than she did, felt differently than she did, and lived differently.

"I've been given a second chance, Father, and I don't know why."

"What do you mean?"

"I had a biopsy that tested positive for a very bad form of cancer; I was a little bit scared, but I was okay. I really was. I've lived a good life and was ready to acknowledge it was over. Then I was told the results were wrong. Specimens had been switched. I was fine." Isabelle had a hard time speaking because of the lump in her throat. "I came to you wondering why God was giving me this second chance, a chance I didn't ask for and am not sure I want." She hoped desperately for a solid response. "I thought maybe you could help me straighten it all out...the odd encounters, the second chance, all of it. Maybe it all works together."

"Perhaps it does, Isabelle. I don't know."

No, this visit was not helpful. Isabelle felt exhausted and defeated. "I think I'd better go now, Father."

"Are you unhappy with me, Isabelle? Are you sorry you came?"

She had always half-believed that priests were endowed with magical powers of a sort and, as if in confirmation, now he was reading her mind. She nodded.

"I know I haven't given you the answers you came here seeking, but that's because I believe you're ready to find them on your own. You don't need what I used to give you. You're strong, Isabelle; you're an amazing woman and you're still growing. I'm proud of you."

No one had said those words to her – about pride – since her father died thirty-three years ago. She looked at her hands, embarrassed to look at the priest. The gnarled knuckles and tissue-thin skin reminded her of her age. She was supposed to be living a peaceful life by now, a cosseted, comfortable life in which others would take care of her. And she had been, until a couple of weeks ago.

* * *

She wasn't at all sure why she found herself back at Phillip Maxwell's bedside. She had expected to leave her visit with Father McGuire feeling better, put back together, as she always had in the past. But this time he had failed her. By affirming her lack of certainty and giving a name to her feeling of vulnerability he had virtually celebrated her weakness.

192

Maybe she was here because Phillip seemed even more helpless than she; maybe it was because he was a cause she could take on, a mission. Maybe she felt that somehow she could regain her footing and sense of herself as a productive member of society if she could help someone. Maybe that's why she was here.

But as she sat by the bed watching Phillip sleep, she wondered why she hadn't just written a big check for some cause, instead. Doing that and throwing extravagant parties for charities had made her feel adequately useful for all these years, so why should she now take this new tack of personal involvement?

"Mrs. Peretti?" Phillip whispered. "Is that you?"

"Yes," she said.

"Do you hate me?"

"No," she said. "You loved my grandson, and I imagine he loved you. Why would I hate you?"

"Because I caused his death."

"No, you didn't. You took him to a place he wanted to go. You let him try something he wanted to try." Isabelle thought about Jake and his zest for life. "He loved trying things. He was always a little bit reckless, which worried me. But looking back, I realize that's what made him happy and made him who he was. His adventures are what made life worth living for him, that and his art."

"And his grandmother," Phillip said weakly.

"Jake was not one to sit home and watch television," Isabelle continued, embarrassment causing her to ignore Phillip's intervention. "He was not one to go to debutante balls or museum openings. He wanted to be out and about, as he put it. He loved the streets, he loved the diversity of the city, and he wanted to experience everything. He once asked me how anyone could live in Manhattan and not want to gobble it all up. Those were his words, 'gobble it all up.'"

"What are you saying?" Phillip asked.

"I guess I'm saying you were only helping him do what he wanted to do, what he probably would have done in any case." She looked out the dirty window at the building next door. "Everyone wanted to make Jake happy; he was irresistible."

"Do you think they'll ever find the person who killed him?" Phillip spoke so softly she could hardly hear him.

"I don't know."

"What would you do if they did?"

"I have no idea," Isabelle said.

"I think I'd try to kill him," Phillip said.

* * *

"Is everything all right, Mother?" Bill gave Isabelle a peck on the cheek as she let him into her suite at the Pierre. "Are you okay?"

"I'm not sure if everything's all right," she said. "That seems to be a more difficult question than it used to be. But I'm fine. I just want to talk. Thank you for coming by."

Bill took off the teal cashmere scarf that matched his plaid shirt and dropped it, along with his camel coat, onto a chair. Isabelle had always admired Bill's willingness to go for bright colors in fashion despite his otherwise generally conservative approach to life. Color was something neither his father nor his brother had indulged in, but Jake had followed Bill's lead and always lit up a room when he walked in.

He sat down in his usual place on the sofa, but Isabelle remained standing. She folded her arms.

"Maybe you should marry her," she said without prologue.

"What are you talking about?"

"You know very well what I'm talking about. Your friend. The one you've been 'seeing.'"

"Larissa," he said. "Her name's Larissa. What made you change your mind about her?"

"I haven't changed my mind about the propriety of the whole thing. It's not something I would do and not something you should be proud of, and it's unfortunate you two couldn't have figured this out when you met, all those years ago, before you were married, but we can't change that now."

"You think I should leave Vanessa?"

"I didn't exactly say that, William." Isabelle sank into the chintz chair she always sat in when her son was here. "I just think maybe you should do what you need to do to be happy, to be fulfilled, to be complete – if it's possible to be complete in this life."

"I've never heard you talk this way before, Mother. What's going on?"

"I had a talk with Father McGuire this morning, and I've come to realize there are things we can't do in eternity, things we can only do now. And I've learned that what's good and bad and right and wrong is not always so clear. And that ultimately we're alone in this life to take care of ourselves and do what we need to do to get by and, if we're lucky, give it all some kind of meaning."

"Father McGuire said that? I still don't quite understand what...."

"No, he didn't exactly say it. I just think that if we find someone special - not just anyone, but someone who truly completes us and makes us less alone - someone to not just go through life with but someone who can maybe even give it meaning, we shouldn't let that person pass by. When you suggested your relationship with this woman Larissa might have a spark of the divine in it, I chided you for bringing God into your sin, but I might have been wrong." The clear night sky out the window was starting to fade into evening darkness, its color not unlike Bill's scarf. "Maybe it's about divinity. Or maybe divinity doesn't even exist. I honestly don't know, William. After all these years, I still haven't figured it out. I don't know if we have a purpose or a role to play in being here, but I do think we need to take heed when something very, very powerful pulls at us."

Bill got up from the sofa and sat on the ottoman at the foot of his mother's chair. He took her worn, frail hands in his strong, elegant ones; Isabelle had always thought he should be a pianist. "I can't believe you're becoming an existentialist at this point in your life, Mother. A Catholic one, at that." He chuckled. "God, I love you so much."

"So, are you going to marry her?" Isabelle said through a lump in her throat.

"I don't know what I'm going to do. I'm not sure she'll have me. I think I may have blown it."

"Why? What did you do?"

"It's more what I didn't do. I haven't had the nerve to actually say I'd leave Vanessa, or my life as I know it. I guess I've been afraid to make that decision. And Larissa's unhappy being in a clandestine relationship with a man she thinks is not fully committed to her."

"It's not hard to understand her point of view," Isabelle said softly. "*Are* you committed to her?"

"Unconditionally," Bill said. "I've loved her since the day I met her; I've never loved anyone more."

"Are you willing to give up your life for her, the life you have in Connecticut with Vanessa?"

Bill dropped Isabelle's hands. He didn't answer.

"Maybe it's not so unconditional, after all."

"But it is," he said. "I can't imagine life without her."

"But you can't seem to imagine life *with* her, either."

"Actually...I can, at least partly." He took Isabelle's hands again, and squeezed them so tightly she felt her finger bones shift. "I've done nothing lately *but* imagine that. I know exactly how it would feel going to bed with her each night and waking up with her in the morning. I know what it would be like drinking coffee and reading the paper together. I know how it would feel to watch her perform, knowing she would be coming home with me. I've imagined all that.

"But I can't quite imagine the rest of the day. I can't imagine the structure of our days...where we'd live, what we'd do all day, how we'd make a life that would please both of us, what it would all look like. I imagine it would be lovely, but I can't imagine the commonplace details.

"And I can't imagine telling Vanessa, or the kids. I know Jeff would understand, and I actually believe Vanessa might be relieved, in some way. But I don't know about Marianne, and there's nothing in the world that would hurt me more than hurting her. Then there are the people at the hospital and the club; I don't know what they'd say or think or how it would affect my relationships with them. I know people do this all the time, but I can't imagine how it would play out in my own life."

Isabelle nodded.

"So, I love Larissa and I want to be with her. That much I know. But I don't know much beyond that, and I'm scared to death of what I don't know." Bill stopped abruptly. "And I don't even know why I'm telling you all this."

"Because I asked," Isabelle said simply. "And because I'm your mother."

Bill laughed.

"You know, I still am," Isabelle said, "even though it has not escaped my notice that the roles have reversed since your father died."

"Oh mother..."

"No, I mean it. I recognize you've been taking care of me, and I appreciate it, William. I really do. Actually, I've quite taken it for granted, for the most part."

"Stop it, Mother. You're very independent...."

"I'm going to stop you before you add, 'for a woman of your age,'" Isabelle said. "I know I'm able to be 'independent' because I'm living in what amounts to a high-class assisted-living facility."

"If you're unhappy here...."

"I didn't say that, William. I love my suite and love having everything done for me here. It's a wonderful hotel, a perfect location, and the staff couldn't be nicer." Isabelle patted Bill on the knee. "This is perfect for a woman like me, one who's always been taken care of."

Bill started to say something, but she cut him off.

"Until very recently, I never thought much about my life. Never thought about how I lived or how I should or how anyone else did. I simply lived according to the rules, according to all the prescriptions and proscriptions that were evident, even those not spoken."

"Are you happy you've done it that way?"

"I'm not unhappy, William. But I'm now beginning to think there's more to it all, that I might have missed something along the way." The sky was now a clear, dark blue.

"How could you have missed anything, Mother? You've traveled the world, you've had all of New York at your fingertips; you've had the means to do whatever you wanted."

"Yes, I've traveled, but everywhere I went I lived exactly as I do here. I was always comfortable and cared for, either ignoring the harsher things or seeing them from a distance. I've done things most people only dream of, I know. I've lived an enviable life. But William, I'm beginning to think I've only skated across the surface of it. I've never really dug in very deeply. Others always protected me from that, and I allowed myself to accept the protection."

"Father protected you because he loved you. Didn't he give your life meaning?"

"We did love each other," Isabelle said, directing a soft glance at her youngest child. "But I'm not sure it was all it might have been, all it could have been."

"What do you mean?"

Isabelle could see she was torturing William with this talk. She knew he wanted her to be happy and couldn't stand to think she might not have been, but she went on. "You, of all people, should understand what I'm talking about...you, with your hopeless, perfect love," she said sadly. "I never had that hopeless feeling with your father, that desperately-in-love feeling. I never had to fight for him, make sacrifices for him, or even consider it. I liked him immensely, I respected him, we were compatible, but there was no passion, William, no feeling of destiny or completion when we were together. It was easy, it was pleasant – delightfully so – but it was never the stuff poetry is written about or wars fought over."

"It makes me sad to hear you say that, Mother.

"I don't want to make you sad, William, I just want to make you think. I don't want you to miss out on what you can only do in this life, what you can't do, no matter how good and holy and righteous you are, in eternity."

Chapter Thirteen: Finding the Essence

Saturday, October 1, 2005

Larissa threw back her head and sang the closing words to "My Way." Her long red hair cascaded past her shoulders and fell loosely down her back, giving her a sense of freedom that complemented the song's words. She was sad but relieved to have taken control of the situation which had dominated her life for nearly two years.

The evening at Picholine had been painful, of course. She had said what she thought she would never be able to say when she told Bill she could no longer stand being consumed by a man whose core commitment lay elsewhere.

When he walked her home that night, she had insisted he leave her outside the front door of the building. When he tried to kiss her goodnight, she had turned away, allowing his lips to touch only her right cheek. That was enough; that was just right. It was the kind of kiss friends give friends, if a little more awkward, and she wanted to believe they could someday be friends. That's how they had begun; that's how they should end. Larissa appreciated symmetry, which is why she didn't like what they had become.

"I love you, Larissa," he had said in a pleading tone of voice, "and I need you. Why are you doing this?"

"Because you don't need me as much as you need other things in your life, and I needed you more than anything."

"But we're so good together."

"We were," she said.

And with that, she had gone inside. She turned and looked back at him as she as she stepped into the elevator; she thought she saw a tear run down his face. It had taken every ounce of strength she possessed to keep from running back outside.

But tonight, as she sang at Bemelmans, she felt good.

She had stopped in after her performance across the hall at the Café Carlyle because she needed the diversion and, yes, the adoration. They particularly loved to see her here when she was the main event at the Café. It made the lounge patrons feel like they were getting a high-priced, SRO show practically for free, which they were.

As she wrapped up "My Kind of Town," a slim, dark-haired man with refined features approached the piano. He handed her a twenty, and quietly asked her to play "Not Exactly Paris." Unlike the Porter, Gershwin, and Cole she was used to playing for requests, this was not a song many people knew, but it was one of her favorites. She nodded at the man, told him to hold onto his money, and began playing.

He sat down at a table near the corner, next to the one Larissa had shared with Bill on the night they had gotten back together. He watched her play, and he smiled a crooked smile.

* * *

John Taylor held the door open for Natalie as they walked into the small, dark room. He'd never been in Bemelmans before, but came by this evening because he'd heard Larissa was likely to be performing. He had tried to get tickets to her late show at the Carlyle, but they were sold out. The maitre d', who had obviously sensed his disappointment, had told him, in the strictest confidence, that she sometimes played an informal gig at Bemelmans after her Café Carlyle performances.

"It's not on the program, and it's not a commitment. She just does it occasionally as kind of a surprise. So, don't say anything about it, and don't count on it, but if you really want to see her you might get lucky, especially on a Saturday night."

He had convinced Natalie to come here after dinner and the theater, plans they had made for tonight before their break-up.

"Why don't we just go through with the evening?" John had said when he called her about it. "You want to see the show, and we've got the tickets."

"I don't know," Natalie had said. "I mean, you call off the wedding and move out, and now you want to go on a *date*? You *dumped* me, John."

The words stung. "I love you, Natalie, but I had to be fair to you. Do we have to go through this all over again?"

"I've been thinking about what you said," she replied, "that we were 'traveling down different roads.' But I still don't get it. I know you want to be a writer; I've always known that. Why wouldn't you believe I could live with that?"

"You need me to be a lawyer, like your father; it's the kind of life you're used to. It's what you're proud of me for. You've told me that. But I want to leave that behind to be a writer *fulltime*. That wouldn't be what you married into. I'm not talking about being Phillip Roth here, or Saul Bellow or Peter Taylor. I'm talking about most likely being pretty obscure and pretty poor. That's no life for you."

"I wish you'd let *me* be the one to decide that," she said.

John didn't know what to say. He thought he had done what was right, even necessary, and he thought she'd come to understand that. More to the point, they'd been through this all too many times before. "So anyway," he had said meekly, "want to go ahead with our Saturday night plans?"

"Why not?" she said with what sounded too much like resignation. "I certainly don't have any others."

Dinner at Felidia had been grand, as always, but the Broadway revival of "Company" had been unsettling in its all-too-relevant depiction of the joys and pains of married life versus the easy emptiness of being alone.

That's why the stop at Bemelmans seemed particularly important. If they got lucky, Larissa would be the perfect antidote to Sondheim. Even though her repertoire generally listed toward sadness, hers were songs with soothing melodies and simple, comprehensible lyrics, the kind that made love and loss accessible, the kind John needed to hear in order to get Sondheim's angular rhythms and complex concepts out of his head.

He put his hand on the small of Natalie's back as they walked into the dark lounge, guiding her in a way that felt as natural as falling asleep. They wound their way between the small tables over to an empty one on the far side of the room, a table in the corner, against the wall, where they could share a banquette and have a view of the piano.

John grinned at Larissa and waved shyly. She was playing a song he didn't know, dreamily immersed in the music. John ordered a glass of cabernet, Natalie asked for a fume blanc.

As they listened to the music and waited for their drinks, John tried not to think about how much he already missed seeing her face the last thing each night and the first thing every morning.

When Larissa finished the number, she got up and came over to their table.

"Well, hello there, John Taylor," she said with a grin. She sat down in the chair opposite him and Natalie. "Who's your friend?"

"This is Natalie," he said, feeling flustered; he was still star-struck in Larissa's presence. "Natalie, this is Larissa."

Larissa stuck out her hand. "Any friend of John Taylor's is a friend of mine," she said, then grimaced. "I suppose I shouldn't talk in clichés in front of a writer."

John laughed nervously, while Natalie shook Larissa's hand awkwardly. Larissa waved to the bartender and ordered a Stoli martini.

"So, tell me, Natalie. How do you know my friend John Taylor?"

Natalie seemed to cast about in her mind for a good answer, ultimately coming up with the simplest one. "We used to be engaged."

Larissa was momentarily stopped by that one.

"...until earlier this week," Natalie continued. "John broke it off."

"I'm....uh...I'm sorry?" Larissa said.

"I am too," Natalie replied.

Larissa looked at John.

"I still love her," he said simply, having no idea what made him say that in this context.

"So, why...?" Larissa started.

"And I love him," Natalie interrupted.

"So....."

"He thinks I need to marry a lawyer."

"He *is* a lawyer," Larissa said.

"He wants to be a writer," Natalie replied.

"I know," Larissa said.

"He doesn't think I can handle that," Natalie said.

"Why not?"

"It's a lifestyle thing," she said. "He doesn't think I could live with a struggling writer."

John had never seen Natalie like this, so forceful, so sort of...confrontational. And he'd never seen her air what her mother would surely call their dirty linen in public.

"I guess you should be the one to decide what kind of life you want," Larissa said, peering over at the attractive man at the next table.

"I couldn't agree more," Natalie said.

Larissa looked at John. "So, John Taylor, what do you think?"

He looked back at Larissa, who was so beautiful tonight in a gold sequined gown, with her red hair shiny and flowing and that peaceful countenance. Then he looked at Natalie who seemed so small and thin, but suddenly so strong and so sure of what she wanted.

"I guess maybe I acted a little too quickly."

"Here-here, John Taylor," Larissa said, lifting her martini in a toast. "It takes a big man to admit a mistake, and a smart one to correct it."

"I guess I'm not as smart as I thought I was," John said, "but I'll try to correct it."

"We'll take our time," Natalie said calmly, "and see where we end up."

* * *

Larissa loved what was happening here, and for the briefest of moments allowed herself to envision a happy ending with Bill. Then she remembered the man sitting at the next table.

"Want to meet my friends?" she said, pulling out her old lounge singer persona.

"I'd love to," the man said quietly. "I wouldn't mind meeting you, as well."

The words sounded like a come-on, but the straightforward tone seemed otherwise.

"I'm Larissa," she said, sticking out her hand. "Larissa Sinclair."

"Jack Flaherty," he said.

Why did she always attract the Irish and Italians?

"Jack Flaherty, this is John Taylor and Natalie," Larissa said. "Why don't you scoot on over here and join us?"

"Are you sure? I don't want to interrupt."

"Of course I'm sure," Larissa said.

Jack moved down the banquette, and joined the group.

"So, what's your story?" Larissa said to Jack.

"My story?"

"Everyone has a story," she said. "Tell us about yourself."

211

"There's not much to tell."

"Where are you from? What do you do? How do you know my favorite song?"

"I'm from right here in New York...a few blocks away. What I do now is mostly collect art. And I know your song because Mickey Leonard is one of my favorite musicians, and I think George Russell wrote a perfect lyric."

"Me too," Larissa said. "I've loved Mickey since I first learned to play the piano."

"He's a genius," Jack said, "and there aren't many people I would say that about."

Larissa nodded. "You collect art?"

"I do."

Larissa was not used to dealing with a man she had to pull information out of. Most were only too anxious to talk about themselves. She rather liked the change. "What kind of art?"

"Mostly minimalist, mostly from the 1970's."

"I don't know much about modern art," Larissa said. "What's minimalist?"

Jack paused as if assessing whether she was pulling his leg or patronizing him, then responded. "It's art that's very simple in style, though not always in concept."

"I'm the same way," Larissa laughed.

"I imagine that's true," Jack said.

"But tell me about your art," she said. "I didn't mean to interrupt."

"I don't want to bore you all," he said.

"You're not boring anybody. Tell us," Larissa said.

"Well, it's mostly stark, hard-edged, geometric, clean-lined. There's not a lot of color, not a lot of busyness. It's simple and reductive and pure, in a way life rarely is. I imagine that's why I find it soothing. It boils the world down to its most basic lines and shapes and volumes. It's sometimes about finding the ultimate reduction, but to me it's simpler than that; it's about finding essences." He stopped himself. "Sorry, I didn't mean to lecture."

"Hardly a lecture," said John Taylor. "This is the first time I've ever heard anyone say anything about minimalism that made sense."

Even Natalie, who had looked mostly bemused since Jack joined them, looked quite content. It was as if just hearing about purity and the essentials from this unusual man had cast a lovely spell over all of them; at least that's the way it seemed to Larissa.

"I have to admit it was foreign to me until my wife got me into it."

Of course, Larissa thought. Of course there was a wife.

"She was the one with the soul in our family."

"So, she's the collector?" Larissa asked gamely.

"She was until she died," Jack said. "We collected together for years. Went all over the world doing it. It was a wonderful shared adventure. Now I do it alone, but I can always hear her voice when I see something I know she'd love. That's what I buy. She had an exquisite eye."

"I'm sorry," Larissa murmured.

Jack shook his head. "We had something most people never find, and we had it for thirty years. I miss her, of course. But I'm grateful." He shook his head, as if clearing it. "Sorry," he said. "I don't know what got me started."

"Don't apologize," Larissa said. "It's the kind of relationship we all need to hear about from time to time. And as it happens, now's exactly the time the three of us needed to hear about it."

"She would have liked you," Jack said, "and your music."

214

"I'm sure I would have liked her too," Larissa said.

"Are you going to play some more?" he asked.

"No, I'm beat," she said. "I did two shows at the Café Carlyle before this. I'm going to get going."

"Do you live nearby?" Jack said.

"Across the park."

"Can I walk you home?" he said. "It's a beautiful night."

Chapter Fourteen: Your Wife is a Very Lucky Woman

Saturday, October 8, 2005

Frank liked working Saturday nights. It got him out, gave him something to do. Working was what he did; a bartender was who he was. That was the long and short of it.

Right after Chloe died his boss had insisted he take two weeks off.

"It's okay," Frank had protested. "I don't need time off; I don't want time off. I don't have anything to do."

"You need time for yourself." His boss had spoken quietly and benevolently, as Frank imagined a shrink would speak. "Time to mourn, to grieve, to rest, time to get your head back together."

"My head's fine," Frank had said. He knew it wasn't, but he also knew that being alone would not straighten it out. "I'm really able to do this; I don't want to leave you short-handed."

"We can manage," his boss had said. And that had ended the conversation.

So, twenty-nine years ago, Frank had taken the only extended vacation of his life.

He slept for two days straight, which was to be expected since he had sat by Chloe's bedside nearly every minute of her final ten days. That sleep, which encompassed two rainy, stormy days and nights, had been a perfect escape and the best rest he had ever had. It had allowed him to dig his way into a deep, dark, still place where he found peace. He didn't have to talk to anyone or do anything. Most importantly, he didn't have to think about anything, like what his place in the universe would now be. Chloe had given him not only love but a purpose, a role, something to care about and live for. He hadn't had that before and didn't imagine ever finding it again.

Then he had woken up. Abruptly. The sleep was over and, hard as he tried to bring it back, it wouldn't return. It was Thursday. Looking out the small, dirty kitchen window over the cloudy Bronx tenement skyline, he had sipped coffee and nibbled on a piece of stale toast. He thought that if he were a stronger person he might try to take his own life, end this existence that now had no meaning. The idea was appealing, but he knew he would never make it happen. His parents had been working class Irish Catholic immigrants, not French philosophers.

He poured another cup of coffee from the aluminum percolator pot and stirred a teaspoon of sugar into it. He generally liked cream in his coffee too, but what he had in the refrigerator was spoiled. That was okay; the coffee's bitter blackness seemed appropriate, though inconsistent with the cheery orange-and-blue floral pattern that adorned the white melamine cup. Chloe had loved these dishes, saying they were both practical and beautiful. Frank had known the Pierre would never use melamine, but he hadn't said anything. Chloe's sweet naiveté was something he cherished. If she loved these dishes she would have them, and he would never spoil it for her.

He spent most of the next twelve days – the balance of his involuntary leave of absence – sitting at that table. Going out seemed like too much of an effort, and he wasn't the kind of man to have anyone in. Chloe had been the spark of life in their marriage, the one who was always out and meeting and talking and making friends. He was happy to let her do it, and to occasionally accompany her, but he didn't indulge in that sort of thing himself, preferring solitude, and justifying it by pointing out how social he had to be at work.

And nothing was different now that she was gone. He simply didn't want anyone around. In fact, he preferred his solitude, and his kitchen table, now more than ever.

Except on Saturday nights. Those were the nights he and Chloe had always gone out. "Our night," she called it. Sometimes it was a movie, sometimes dinner with friends, sometimes bowling. It didn't matter. The idea was to be out and together. She loved the out; he loved the together. So, Saturday nights had been special.

They had meant so much to Chloe that Frank had made free Saturday nights a condition of his early employment at the Pierre. The powers-that-be had agreed to it because he was a damn good bartender who came from the Algonquin with stunning references. It didn't hurt that most of the Pierre's other staff were older and didn't really care about free Saturday nights.

But ever since the conclusion of his two-week exile, twenty-nine years ago, Frank had insisted on working Saturday nights. That was the one night he still, to this day, could not stand being at home alone.

* * *

Tonight's crowd was on the quiet side. It was a mostly benign, anonymous group, aside from two spillover Monday night regulars, the woman from Yale named Gloria and the gentle jazzman who resembled August Wilson. So, Frank's job had been mostly restricted to mixing and occasionally delivering drinks. Not too much handholding or coddling had been required, and he was rather enjoying the relative serenity.

But then Mike came in, the man with the unique ability to send a chill down Frank's spine, and not metaphorically. He swaggered – and staggered – through the Café Pierre's front door, walked straight over to the bar, and pulled off his leather bomber jacket. He draped it across the back of the bar stool next to Gloria's, surreptitiously admiring the rippling of his bicep tattoos as he leaned over the bar. He barked out an order for aquavit.

"Make it a triple," he said loudly.

"How's it going, baby?" he asked Gloria.

"Okay," she replied, "but I could use another Manhattan. This one's about gone, and I'm not nearly drunk enough to go home yet."

"Bring another one for the lady, Frankie," Mike said.

Frank hated being called "Frankie" by this lunatic, but he was nothing if not the consummate professional, so he filled the orders and kept quiet.

* * *

"How'd you like to come home with me, Glo?" Mike said to Gloria, after downing three triples. He was beginning to slur his words.

221

He'd been sidling up to her all evening, but not saying much or paying much attention as she droned on and on about herself and her tragic life. Frank felt like he should give the guy a tip for taking her off his hands.

"That's not gonna happen," Gloria mumbled. She'd put away four or five drinks herself and was even less articulate than usual. Then she chuckled.

"What the hell's so funny," Mike shouted. Heads turned to see what the commotion was all about.

Clearly too drunk to be intimidated, Gloria chuckled some more. "The thought of *me* coming home with *you*." Her fat red lips turned up at the corners, making her cheeks pouch out. "Why the hell would I do that?"

Mike slammed a tightly clenched fist down on the bar. "What's that supposed to mean?" The look on his face scared the hell out of Frank.

Gloria chuckled some more. Frank wanted to tell her to quit it, to shut up, but instinct told him to stay out of it.

"It means just that. Why the hell would I want to come home with you?"

Mike pulled back his hand as if preparing to slap her; Gloria ducked and let out a little shriek. Mike looked at Frank, then down the bar at all the other people who were watching him, and let his arm drop back to his side. "I can tell you're attracted to me," he said quietly to Gloria. "You don't want to admit it."

Frank was relieved to see that by now she was smart enough not to chuckle.

"You're attracted to me," Mike said, "because I'm the kind of guy who makes things happen. I don't sit around and take what the world dishes out. I'm an in-charge kind of guy. I don't whine about my past or my problems the way you do. I don't bitch about the way the world's treated me. If I have an issue, I deal with it.

"Give me another," Mike said, motioning to Frank with his empty glass.

Frank was reluctant to give the refill but afraid not to. He poured the last of the aquavit from the bottle, realizing Mike had downed practically the whole thing. He took the empty glass from the bar and replaced it with the full one.

Mike took a big swig and slammed the glass down on the bar. "You don't believe me, do you?" he said to Gloria.

"Believe what?" she said.

"That I take care of my issues."

She shrugged. "How would I know?"

He moved closer to her, so that his mouth was no more than a couple of inches from her nose. "I killed a guy," he said quietly, but not so quietly that Frank didn't hear.

Gloria seemed more curious than shocked. "That so?"

Mike nodded. "Faggot."

"You killed a gay guy?" Gloria said, holding her empty glass out toward Frank for a refill.

Mike nodded again, a smug grin plastered across his face.

"Why?" she asked.

"Revenge."

"He messed with you?"

"Not exactly. His friend messed with my brother. Different kind of revenge."

Frank was relieved that no one else in the place seemed tuned in on the conversation at that point; he'd call in security as soon as he could step away. He set Gloria's drink down in front of her.

She sipped it, then said, "How'd you do it?"

"You don't want to know the details, baby. Suffice it to say I made my point, and pretty well took care of his in the process." Mike laughed loudly. "Yep, pretty well...."

"Did you use a gun?"

"Knife," Mike said. "Right here in the park...right over where the fags congregate. The guy pretty much set himself up for me, made himself a perfect target."

"Who was the guy?" Gloria asked.

"Artist. You probably heard about it on TV. Big story."

"When?"

"While back. Maybe you weren't in town yet. Last winter."

Frank felt like he was going to lose his lunch. This asshole had killed Isabelle's grandson, unless he was making it all up as some sick form of self-aggrandizement. He moved away from the bar, trying to appear casual.

He walked across the Rotunda and down the long corridor to the lobby where he found Angus, the plain-clothes security man, talking with one of the front desk staff. Frank told him what he'd overheard.

"I'll call the cops," Angus said, "but we've got to get the guy out of the bar. You know whose heads are going to roll if the folks upstairs hear we made a scene in the hotel."

Frank nodded.

"If you can get him to step outside, I'll make sure the cops meet him there."

So, Frank went out the lobby door, took in the cool night air for a minute to clear his head, then went around to the Café entrance and waited for the cops to arrive. As soon as they pulled up in front of the Café's gold and white awning, Angus appeared and nodded to Frank. "Get him out here."

Frank walked up to the bar and approached Mike. "You're Mike, right?" After all this time, they'd never actually been introduced.

"'Course."

"A friend of yours is waiting outside," Frank said. "She says she doesn't want to come in."

Mike looked puzzled but pleased, no doubt glad to have Gloria hear that a woman was here for him. "Be right back...maybe," he said to Gloria with a wink. And he walked out the door.

* * *

226

"Thanks for your help." The policeman came back to the bar several hours later, when Frank was in the process of closing up. "He seems to be our guy. He's not just confessing, he's bragging. Pathetic little fucker."

"How do you know he's not some insane guy who read about the murder and decided he'd like the glory?" Frank said.

"He knew some pretty important facts that hadn't been publicized, and everything he said jibed with what we know, not that I'm pre-judging." He gave Frank a big, sarcastic grin. "Innocent 'til proven guilty, of course."

"Will you notify the kid's family...the one who was murdered?" Frank said.

"Yeah, we'll let the parents know. Probably in the morning."

"Kid's grandmother lives here at the hotel," Frank said.

"No kidding," the cop said, taking in the posh surroundings. "Good life."

Frank nodded. "Mind if I tell her about this? I don't want her to read it in the paper or see it on TV."

"It shouldn't be out there; we probably won't make a release tonight. But you never know. Could leak. The press's been all over this one."

"So, can I tell her?" Frank persisted. "She's old, and a little...fragile, if you know what I mean." He wasn't sure why he felt so protective of Isabelle, but the fact was he did.

"I really can't keep you from doing that, can I," the cop said matter-of-factly. "Just don't go blabbing it all over town."

"Don't worry," Frank said. "And my bosses would appreciate it if you didn't make a big deal of where the guy was when he started bragging tonight...know what I mean?"

"I'll see what I can do," the cop said, heaving himself off the barstool. "Thanks again, pal." And he lumbered out of the Café.

* * *

Frank picked up a house phone and asked the operator to connect him to Mrs. Peretti's room.

"Hello? Who *is* this?"

Frank could tell from those few words that he'd roused Isabelle from sleep and that she was afraid. He recalled her telling him about the late-night call she had gotten when Jake was killed.

"It's me, Frank...the bartender downstairs," he said. "Can I come up for a minute? There's something I need to tell you."

There was silence at the other end of the phone.

"You there, Mrs. P?

"It's two o'clock in the morning. Can't you tell me by phone?"

"I'd rather tell you in person."

Another long pause. "Is this really necessary? I'm not dressed."

"I can wait," Frank said.

He heard a long sigh. "Give me ten minutes," she said.

* * *

Isabelle came to the door in a full-length blue silk robe and satin slippers. She had obviously taken time to pull her hair back into its usual neat bun and put on a little face powder, tiny tan flecks of which spotted the robe's lapel. She showed Frank into the living room.

The view of the park at night with the lights of Central Park West across the way, all lit by a full moon, was breathtaking. Frank couldn't help thinking about his own view across to the public housing complex with its graffitied walls and barred windows.

Isabelle motioned for him to sit on the sofa, which he did.

Not knowing how to say what he had to say, he just said it. "The police have arrested a man they think murdered your grandson."

Isabelle's small body sank heavily into an overstuffed chair. "Who?" she said. "How do you know?"

"His name is Mike; he was in the bar downstairs."

"How did they know?"

"He talked about it."

"He confessed?"

Frank nodded.

"Why are you telling me this?"

"Because I didn't want you to read about it or see it on TV. That didn't seem right."

Her mouth opened a crack. She took a deep breath and said, "Thank you. You're a good man."

Frank shook his head, not sure what he was denying. "I'm sorry about this, Mrs. Peretti, sorry you have to go through this."

"I've already gone through it," she said very slowly. "Jake's dead; he's not coming back. I've learned that. I'll never understand it, but I know it and I've dealt with it. This is something else entirely. This is, maybe, what they call justice being done, although it's hard for me to use that word in this context."

Frank was amazed at her calm.

"There really is no justice in this whole thing," she continued, musing. "I don't think life is about people getting what they deserve. It's much simpler than that; it's about things happening to you and about dealing with them when they do, because things are going to happen. The tragedy of Jake's life is that it was so short, way too short, but he dealt with every aspect of if magnificently."

"Is there anything I can do for you, Mrs. Peretti?" Frank said.

"You've already done me a great service by coming up here and delivering this news. That can't have been easy," she said. "You have been so good to me, talking with me, listening to me, helping me deal with some of the most confusing things I've ever had to cope with. Who would have ever thought a bartender would be so much more helpful to me than my priest?"

Frank laughed, not knowing what else to do. He felt his face flush.

"I mean it," Isabelle said earnestly. "You are a fine man. Your wife is a very lucky woman."

Frank supposed she said that because he still wore his wedding band; he'd never taken it off, and he never would.

* * *

Morning was beginning to dawn by the time Frank got home. He made himself a pot of coffee and watched the sun come up, noticing that the first rays of sun filtering through the dirty window pane were actually

231

quite interesting, even beautiful, more so than when they glinted off sparkly, clean glass.

He really wanted to believe what Mrs. Peretti had said about him helping her. It felt good, different from the services he usually performed. For the first time in twenty-nine years he felt like Chloe might really be proud of him, and even though he wasn't the kind of guy who usually thought this way, he kind of hoped she had been watching.

Chapter Fifteen: I've Done it for You

Saturday, October 15, 2005

Larissa dug through her jewelry box on Saturday evening, searching for the dangly gold earrings she liked to wear with her red Valentino dress. She wanted to look chic but not too slinky for her date with Jack Flaherty, if "date" was even the correct term for it. He was taking her to an opening at the PaceWildenstein Gallery, a place she'd never been.

She hadn't seen Jack in the two weeks since they had met at Bemelmans, but they had talked on the phone five or six times. He seemed a little shy, she thought, or maybe cautious. For whatever reason, he apparently wanted to get to know her from a distance before actually taking her out, which was a concept Larissa found charming. Her usual experience with men was the opposite: they wanted to get to know her physically, and only later – if at all – did an intellectual relationship enter into the equation.

As she combed through the trinkets and bling in her jewelry box, she came across the diamond stud earrings Bill had given her last year. He, of course, had been the exception to the rule. Having started as

233

friends, they only later became lovers. Before the little pang she felt could grow into anything larger, she tossed the diamonds back into the general mélange and continued her search for the gold dangles.

* * *

The exhibit at PaceWildenstein was fascinating. It consisted of sculptures which had been fashioned from cut, crumpled and painted automobile body parts. Some were relatively small, maybe three or four feet high; others were monumental conglomerations and webs of brilliant tone and texture so large Larissa felt like she could get lost inside of them.

"Who would have ever thought you could make junk into art?" she said, as they walked through the show.

"It actually happens a lot," Jack said.

"Kind of like the Ugly Duckling," Larissa said as she examined a work made of twisted ribbons of metal fashioned into a hedge-like structure that must have been fifteen feet long. "This stuff starts in a junkyard, is somehow magically transformed into something beautiful, and ends up in a fancy Upper East Side gallery."

"It's a good analogy, the Ugly Duckling," Jack said. "I'd never quite thought of it that way before, but pretty much all art starts out as very basic, inherently uninteresting and not particularly beautiful materials, like metal, paint, canvas, clay, stone, and earth. The art only happens when the materials are manipulated."

Larissa was happy talking to this man who took her seriously. She was enjoying both the gallery and the company. She linked her arm into Jack's and continued her stroll through the exhibit.

* * *

After dinner at La Goulue on Madison Avenue, Jack walked Larissa back to her apartment, where he gave her a chaste kiss on the lips.

"You are a most unusual woman," he said, holding her by the shoulders and examining her face. "I enjoyed myself immensely this evening. Thank you for coming out with me."

"My pleasure," Larissa said. "Would you like to come up for a nightcap?"

"Thanks," Jack said, "but I'd better be on my way. Rain check?"

"Of course."

Larissa went up to her apartment and took off her makeup and the red dress. She slipped into her favorite soft, jersey pajamas, and opened the freezer to get the bottle of Stoli Raspberry. Then she closed it, deciding she'd rather have a cup of green tea.

While it steeped, she checked her voicemail. There was only one message.

I need to see you, Larissa. Can I come by? Give me a call, okay? On my cell. Anytime, but please make it tonight. I'll be waiting. I really need to see you.

Larissa replayed Bill's message, then carefully replaced the phone's receiver.

Bill had always been the one to call. She couldn't remember him ever asking her to call him back; that wasn't part of their m.o. She was a little frightened, both of what must be wrong in Bill's world to provoke such an unusual request and of the feelings that talking to him or seeing him would likely dredge up. She needed more time and distance – a lot more of both – before she would feel safe communicating with him. She had promised herself she would maintain the necessary separation for as long as it took.

But he sounded so desperate. No, that was an exaggeration. But he *did* sound like he needed to talk. And they *were* friends. She had told him – and herself – that they should always remain friends. That seemed right; it acknowledged the history and the undeniable connection, and seemed like the relationship they were meant to have. So, when a friend calls and needs you, she reasoned...

Even though she knew it was pure rationalization, she picked up the phone and dialed Bill's cell number. He answered on the first ring.

"What do you need to talk about?" she asked.

"I need to see you. Can I come by?"

"Let's talk on the phone."

"I can't do this by phone. Please...."

"Do we have to....?" she said.

"We do," he said. "*I* do. Please?"

"Okay," she said. "Tomorrow."

"Tonight," he said. "Now. I'm staying at the Carlyle; I can be there in ten minutes."

"Why are you doing this to me?"

"I'll tell you everything when I see you."

* * *

He arrived fifteen minutes after they'd hung up. Larissa hadn't bothered changing out of her pajamas or even putting on makeup.

"You look beautiful," he said when she opened the door.

"Stop it, Bill. I look like I was about to get into bed. Because I was." She let him in and offered him a drink.

"Gin and tonic?" he said as he reached out to take her in his arms.

She dodged his advance. "I've still got your Sapphire," she said, and invited him to sit on the sofa while she went to the bar and mixed his drink.

"Sorry, no limes." She handed him the glass.

"As if I care," he said. "What's wrong with you?"

How could he not know?

He lifted his glass. "Aren't you having anything?"

"I'm fine," she said, still standing. She knew she'd lose her resolve if she sat down with him and started drinking. She'd be right back where she'd been before. "Just tell me what this is about."

"I've left," he said.

"What do you mean?" she said, hoping he didn't mean what she was pretty sure he did.

"I've left Vanessa. I've left Greenwich. I've left my old life. That's what I mean."

Larissa stared at him. "Why?" she managed to say.

"Oh God, Larissa. I think you know...."

"I mean, I told you I can't do this...."

"You told me you couldn't do this because you didn't really have me, because I wasn't willing to give up the rest of my life for you. Well, I've done it," he said slowly, enunciating every word of the last sentence. "I've done it for you."

"Why didn't you talk to me first?"

"What are you saying?" he said. "Isn't this what you want? Aren't you happy? We can be together now. *Really* together. I love you so much."

Larissa dropped into the big yellow armchair beside the sofa. She slumped over and put her head in her hands.

"You told me this was what you needed," he said.

"But you can't just *do* that, tell me about it after the fact, and expect me to jump into your arms and say everything's fine and I'm all yours now."

"Why can't I? I thought...."

"Because you can't do that to someone," she said, hating how inarticulate she sounded. "I'm doing okay on my own."

"But I'm here for you now. All of me," he said. "You don't have to be alone."

239

"You aren't listening," she said sadly.

"Oh, Jesus," Bill said. "I really can't believe that this is happening."

"That what's happening?"

"That I've done what I've done for you, and you don't want me, after all."

"I didn't say that. I've always wanted you, and you've always known it. But I need to get my *self* back. I need to get out from under your spell so I can make decisions like this on my own. I don't want to do this just because you tell me you're suddenly ready. That doesn't mean *I'm* ready."

"Don't you love me?"

"Of course I do," she said. "But that doesn't mean I'm ready to jump into something so big and life-changing just because *you've* decided it's time. You can't keep doing this to me."

"I thought I was doing what you wanted," he said.

"I know you did." She moved over to sit beside him on the sofa. "But maybe you were doing what *you* wanted to do about your marriage. And I truly hope you did." She put her hand on his arm and squeezed it. "I'm crazy about you, Bill. I'm always going to be crazy about you. But I have to think about all this. It's never been presented as anything but hypothetical, so I've never really thought it all through."

"Is there someone else?" he asked.

"As a matter of fact, I was out tonight with an awfully nice man, but that's *not* what this is about. This is about me figuring out what's right for me, now that you've figured out what's right for you."

"Are you dumping me?" he said.

"Bill, *listen* to me. I said I love you, and I'll always love you, whatever form that love may take. I'm happy we can see each other and be together now without the guilt and deception. But if you're talking about a long-term, committed, monogamous relationship..."

"I'm talking about marriage, for God's sake," he said.

"...then I need to figure out what's right for me," Larissa concluded quietly.

He had nothing to say.

"Will you be patient with me while I work it out?" she said softly. "And will you respect and support what's right for me, as well as what's right for you?"

His lower lip trembled as he seemed to ponder the question, and he nodded almost imperceptibly. Larissa felt like the meanest person alive. She knew she loved this man, and she knew she'd just hurt him very deeply, but right now she didn't know much of anything beyond that.

Chapter Sixteen: I'd Like You To Have This

Sunday, October 9, 2005

Isabelle stepped out of the taxi in front of Jake's building. She looked at the quiet sidewalks littered with papers, cigarette butts, a bottle or two and even a used condom; she now recognized the detritus as indicators that a vibrant sort of life was lived here. She looked at the scruffy industrial buildings with their steel mesh window-covers and thought about the pristine, white-walled galleries she now knew were hidden behind them. She looked at the broad windows of Jake's loft building and thought about the creative energy she now knew buzzed within. And she looked at the man who slept on the doorstep of the building next door, the man who twitched and groaned and reeked and kept his world in a Bed, Bath and Beyond shopping cart, the man she now knew had a name. Sam.

Isabelle had gotten up at 8:30 this morning, just as she did every Sunday. She had scanned the *Times* and read a Shakespeare sonnet, just as she did every Sunday. She had eaten shirred eggs and toast in the Café Pierre's rotunda, just as she did every Sunday. But she had not attended mass. It's not that she had given up on God, not by any means. She just

243

felt the need to try living for a week without the help of a priest. She wanted to see if she could do it all on her own.

It was unsettling, this small break in what had been her routine for so many years, but it was also liberating, in its way. As she walked up to Jake's building, she thought about how life was negotiable, nothing was set in stone. Just because something was the way it always had been didn't mean it would or could or had to be that way in the future. Nothing was certain, which was scary, and nothing was fixed, which was interesting. It was a whole new concept for her.

As she was about to put her key in the building's front door lock, she noticed Sam was starting to wake up. He gingerly stretched one arm, then the other. He shook his legs as if to release the tension of a night's sleep on the stoop.

She walked over to him.

"Good morning, Sam," she said. His white Styrofoam cup was nowhere to be seen; apparently Sunday was his day off. Isabelle took a twenty-dollar bill from her purse, folded it carefully, and held it out to him.

Sam reached for it with a hand that was dry and cracked. Fissures filled with lines of dried blood ran along the pads of his fingers. "Thank you," he mumbled, and stuffed the bill quickly into the pocket of his rank, soiled khaki pants as if he was afraid she might change her mind and want it back.

"You're welcome," Isabelle replied and started to walk away. But before she had gone more than a few feet she turned back and said, "Do you need anything?"

He didn't respond.

"Is there anything I can do for you?"

He shook his head, and Isabelle headed back to Jake's building.

* * *

Phillip arrived at noon, as Isabelle had requested. He wore red slacks, a bright yellow shirt, and a red sweater. His hair was teased into a high style, and his face was adorned with powder, blush, mascara, shadow and liner. Though Isabelle thought he resembled a clown, she was pleased to see him looking so much brighter, indeed so much more *alive,* than he had in the hospital.

"Come in," she said, ushering him into the loft.

He walked across the threshold and stopped. "God," he whispered, "this place is filled with so many memories." He wiped away a tear. "No one loved him more than we did," he said, "you and I."

"Perhaps," Isabelle said.

245

"I can't believe they caught the bastard who..." Phillip whispered. "I can't believe it was Chad's brother." He sat down on the one hard metal chair in the studio, as if in penance. "My love really *was* fatal," he said, way too dramatically.

"Stop it," Isabelle said. "Love is love. We can't control it, and we can't always control its consequences." Although those words of exoneration would have been anathema to her only a week or two ago, she didn't waver. "The man who killed Jake was a sick, pathetic, despicable character. He did this; you didn't. The sooner you learn the whole world doesn't revolve around you and isn't responding to your actions the better off you'll be."

Phillip's mouth hung half-open as if he had been slapped. "You're amazing," he said.

She shook her head. "Here." She held out the new key to Jake's loft.

"What's this?"

"I own this place, and I have no use for it. I know it means a lot to you. I believe Jake would have been happy knowing you have his space and his art. Do with them what you will."

Phillip's mouth moved but no words came out.

"I'd just like two things," Isabelle continued. "I've always loved that painting." She gestured to a canvas that was at least six feet high and five across. "It reminds me of him." The wispy, brilliantly colored lines that floated across the canvas were reminiscent of a late De Kooning. "It's got his spark. It's delicate and bold, like he was, sweet and tough at the same time. I'd like to have that," she said, "and the gold cross I gave him for his First Communion. He told me last year he still wore it when he was feeling frightened or insecure. He said it still had the power to give him strength. I'd like those two things. Everything else is yours."

* * *

She left Phillip in the loft, sobbing and protesting that she was too, too generous. He was an unusually emotive soul, she thought, and a most peculiar man. But she believed he might have the capacity to be happy, and helping him realize it was important to her, though she didn't know why.

She walked back into the sunshine of 21st Street and across to the stoop where Sam sat nibbling on a Snickers bar and staring out at the building across the street. As she approached, he squinted as if puzzled about who she was and why she was there. He took another bite of his Snickers.

"I'd like you to have this," Isabelle said, pulling the gold cross from her purse and holding it up so Sam could see it. She tried awkwardly to place the chain around his thick neck, but he lurched at her touch.

"I'm sorry," she said, taking a step back. "I didn't mean to scare you...or offend you."

Sam finally held out his hand. She placed the cross in his palm and let the gold chain pool around it like shimmery water. He closed his hand into a tight fist.

"Goodbye, Sam," she said. Then she turned and walked away, taking a last glance at Jake's building before walking over to Tenth Avenue to hail a taxi for the Pierre.

Judy Pomeranz is a freelance writer of art reviews, articles, short stories, novellas and essays which have been published in a wide variety of publications, and an instructor of fiction writing. She is also a lecturer on art history topics, a study leader on art travel tours, and an art advisor who assists clients in finding and procuring works of art and in forming collections. She has taught classes on writing fiction and criticism in Georgetown University's School of Continuing Studies, the Smithsonian Associates Program, the Trinity College Elderhostel Program, and privately. Her short stories and essays have appeared in Crescent Review, Santa Barbara Review, Potomac Review, Fodderwing, élan, and Mass Ave Review, and in the short story anthologies Extreme Gravity, Great Writers, Great Stories, Chesapeake Crimes, and Chesapeake Crimes II.

The photographs on the front and back cover are courtesy of Michael Reynolds. An earlier version of this book, called On the Far Edge of Love: New York Stories, appeared as a serial in élan magazine.

Miniver Press is a publisher of lively and informative ebooks and print books, available on Amazon and at miniverpress.com